ONE
with the
BLUE

JAMES VALVANO

PublishAmerica
Baltimore

Hardcover 978-1-4512-6603-0
Softcover 978-1-4512-6604-7
PUBLISHED BY PUBLISHAMERICA, LLLP
www.publishamerica.com
Baltimore

Printed in the United States of America

To my parents—Joseph and Amelia Valvano:
Your strength and never ending love are my everyday blessings.
Without you, I could not love life the way I do!

In a split second, it comes for us—change. IT alters the very core of our world, especially when the change is drastic and life altering. Each of us reacts to change in various ways. Most of us are blind creatures of habit, and adhere to what we know, afraid to face it head-on. A vast majority of us buries our heads in the sand, decidedly submissive, and allows life to live us. It is characteristically human to live in the moment and remain unprepared for life altering situations. The only thing more powerful than change, is the indisputable fact that we must accept it. Without question, change will come.

Then there are the brave—the ones who strive to conquer the highest mountains, or ride out the perfect storms. I speak not of foolish daredevils, but of the special ones. I speak of the ones who are dealt change, accept it, yet never submit to it. They never allow IT to break them. I speak of the ones who face the furious lion and accept his roar, but ultimately learn to tame him. I speak of the ones who in the face of uncertainty—love more, feel more, and smile more. Those are the ones. They are the brave ones.

James T. Valvano

Beforehand

James already believed the test results would come back positive. I needed to be honest with myself; I believed it too. I had witnessed the onset of the disease, but unfortunately neither one of us knew what it was. For almost ten years, the right side of his body would jerk and tick when he became tired or stressed. Throughout the years, the abnormal movements became more frequent throughout the day. His bouts with depression, anxiety, and paranoia, continued to intensify without a clear cause. His short-term memory was slipping slowly, and he became clumsier. The disease would have remained a mystery, had it not been for John's diagnosis. James' brother John was further along into the progression, and his behavior and mental state became too overwhelming for him to continue to reside with their parents. John was moved to a Group Home soon after, and received the necessary treatment and medications to mask the physical effects of the disease. Although the jerking, unsteady gait, and behavioral outbursts were under control, unfortunately for John, the disease interfered with his daily living and social interactions. John's memory was depleting, and rapidly he was heading toward dementia. James and I visited John often, and when it came time to leave the Group Home, James became detached, depressed, and quiet. Looking back, James would often say that visiting John was his own personal penance. He constantly felt guilty for not spending enough time with John prior to the diagnosis. He hated seeing his brother's decline. I tried to make James see that this was his final chance to have a relationship with John, and in no way should he punish himself or feel guilty.

As we waited for James' test results, I tried to keep his mind occupied. I had taken him to the movie theater and to dinner more than we ever had. James' emotional and mental stability became more erratic, so I tried to keep things calm and stress free. However, that was a while ago. It was difficult, but I had to make decisions for James. I had to place my partner and best friend of fifteen years into a medical facility. It was my only choice. It was my last hope.

James used to tell me—

"When it's my time, I want everyone to understand that my life has been amazing. I have loved deeply, and played hard! I regret nothing, and I want everyone to live life like there's no tomorrow! Tell them to cry a little, and then get over it! I'll be dead for Christ's sake, but not gone!"

In the end, I found his journal. I held on to it and never shared it with another person. Now, I wish to share a portion of it with you. Here is his journey.

January 21, 2009
Wednesday—9:45PM

I am finally able to write. It took some time to use my hands, so I asked Ian to bring me this notebook. He hid it at the bottom of a grocery bag, and it safely made its way to me under the radar. It has been difficult to get to where I am right now. Something inside of me urges me to write, and I am not going to fight it. I feel different. I feel something coming. Whoever reads this might think I am crazy. Some might not. Nevertheless, I need to write everything down and see where it takes me. I have nothing to lose.

I will never forget the crystal blue water. It was warm. It was so comfortably warm. I did not have to swim; everywhere I looked, it was as if an invisible hand carried me along effortlessly. Everywhere I was taken, beauty widened in all directions. Magnificent and majestic colors continued across a wide expanse. I was one with the ocean and it held me within its immense grasp. Any concept of fear was gone and in its place, a womb of peace and serenity cocooned my body. I was a drifting spirit in the midst of such an infinite array of sea life, and a witness to the splendor and tranquility of its ever-growing hypnotic way. That was the first time I saw him. From below, he swam with such ease, and it was in that instant I felt the connection. He was a Harbor Seal—a soft silver coat with dark brown spots. He began to ascend toward me as *the hand* in the water held me securely in place. I experienced a moment of unwavering intoxication and closed my eyes. I felt the water encircle my body as he swam swiftly around me. He then rested his head on my shoulder; his tenderness was almost humanlike. Suddenly, I felt myself surfacing. The ocean's hand released me, and like a balloon, my body lifted upward. I did not want to leave the comforting adoration of the ocean's arms. I looked down to see my seal, but he was gone. I could not understand the pain within my heart, but our connection was broken. Just moments ago, my entire body was at peace, and now pain and stiffness slowly began to emerge.

James, I am here with you.

I heard the soft voice of a woman. The voice was inside my head.

I have been here waiting for you.

I peeled back my eyelids, but everything was blurry. I could barely see her, but she was looking down at me. Am I dead? Am I dreaming?

Do not worry. I will always be here.

I felt calm in her presence. It was very strange, but very tranquil. Although blurred, I could see that she was dressed in white. She was so angelic.

You will remember. You will remember all of it soon…be patient…

Her voice was gone, and I slipped into a dark chasm. I saw myself walking past the receptionist, back out into the waiting room. The Neurologist's office remained cluttered with patients waiting to see the doctor. Staggered within the lobby, I felt their eyes looking. They were staring. I could hear their whispering voices. I was no longer ashamed of the awkward ticking of my right arm. After waiting eleven days, Doctor Spinzer gave me the results. I had my car keys in one hand as I pushed open the glass door and exited the doctor's office. The air was poisoned with the typical Florida humidity. I could hear Dr. Spinzer's words inside my head.

I am sorry Mr. Valvano. The test results are not good. You have a neurological disease and unfortunately, it is terminal. I am sorry…

Suddenly, I was in my vehicle. I pulled onto Fairview Drive with my hands firmly gripping the steering wheel of my 1996 Ford Explorer. I had to get it together and focus. My own thoughts ran rampant.

You just received the worst possible news...

The light turned red and I sat idle behind two vehicles. The silver minivan directly in front of me was full of balloons—red, white, yellow, and blue balloons. I turned away to notice the most intriguing Queen Palm. It stood firmly planted on the opposite corner of Hall and Fairview. It was so perfect. It stood at least twenty feet tall, and its fronds extended like welcoming arms.

...the test results are not good...I am sorry...it is terminal...the results are not good.

The first car made a right onto Hall Avenue, and the balloon-filled minivan followed suit.

I am sorry Mr. Valvano...neurological disease...terminal...terminal...

I felt nothing at first, and then my Explorer began to topple toward the left. In slow motion, glass streamed across from the passenger-side window. Tiny little darts of fragmented window entered my entire right side. All sound ceased to exist. One moment I could see the road, then the sky. I felt no pain. In an acrobatic display, my vehicle tumbled and tumbled, as I remained trapped inside.

Neurological disease...terminal...Mr. Valvano...I am sorry.

***

The Explorer finished its aerial ballet and slammed down hard on the driver's side. I felt the left side of my head hit the pavement through the glassless window. Before slipping away, it happened.

Terminal...Terminal...

For the first time in years, my body was calm. I felt the ticking end as I drifted away. Slowly, so slowly, I was gone.

They will be here soon.

Her soft voice echoed within my ears and broke me from the vision. I was now back in the hospital room with a woman I had never met, but with whom I felt a deep connection. I did not understand it at all, so much was confusing, but the pain was immerging. Slowly I felt everything coming back…then more pain…more pain…

She closed her eyes and kept them shut.

Is she praying?

I looked down at my body, shrouded in the customary hospital attire. I felt tubes within my nose, and I looked up to follow the hanging drip bag down to my left arm. Inches away I noticed the call button controller coiled around the arm-rail of the bed. I turned to peer up at her, but her eyes remained closed. Suddenly, I heard the sound of a monitor "beep" steadily, then more rapidly.

They are coming.

I looked up at her and wanted to know her name. I felt my throat dry and sore, and there was no way I could unearth the words. The woman's eyes opened and she whispered softly.

James, my name is Jade. I will see you soon.

Suddenly I heard frantic footsteps outside the hospital room. At that moment, it reminded me of footsteps you would here as anxious children entered their living rooms on Christmas morning, eager to see how many gifts Santa had left for them. I could not see the door. A white drape made a semi-circle around the bed, blocking my view. I heard the door open, and a nurse bluntly shouted a directive to have Dr. Swartz paged. I looked up as the nurse pulled back the white drape along its track in the ceiling.

"Mr. Valvano?" A heavyset nurse with a tight perm looked down at me. "Don't try to speak, just relax." She did everything she could to keep my attention.

***

She looked over her shoulder and barked at a male nurse who was wheeling in some type of machine. "The page…did anyone page him…let's go…stat, stat."

The male nurse left the machine at the foot of the bed and made his way to the door. "Working on it now Ms. Clemins."

She whispered back to the male nurse. "He might stay awake this time."

I wanted to talk. I wanted to say something. I turned to look at the woman named Jade, but she was gone. More discomfort entered my consciousness. I felt something attached to the left side of my head but could not move my arm to examine it. Then I felt an awkward sensation below my midsection—a catheter.

"Stay with me Mr. Valvano." Nurse Clemins gently requested, as she methodically placed multiple wires and probes onto my head and torso. "The Doctor is on his way…"

Where is she? The woman named Jade.

I wanted so desperately to ask the nurse if she had seen Jade, but words of any kind escaped me. I wanted to speak, but my voice did not exist.

The male nurse rushed back into the room. "Doctor Swartz is on his way…two minutes." His breath was heavy and hard.

Nurse Clemins poked and prodded while the machine steadily took readings of some kind. She looked down at me and gave a heartfelt smile. She could see I was uncomfortable, and noticed that I was looking down at my groin.

"Honey, I know it's uncomfortable. It will be okay, just stay calm."

The pain was a kind I had never experienced. At that moment, I just wanted to die. I wanted to be released from the agony and torture. I closed my eyes and let the tears fall. I wished that I could drift back to the water, the only place I wanted to be. I wanted to understand why I could not stay. I will have to wait to see Jade again, and hope that she will explain.

FLASH

My eyes were painted by a beam of light. It came hard and fast. Moments later, it felt like my head was under water, and I was looking down into a black hole. My eyes began to adjust and from within the darkness, I saw little flickering lights drizzling downward. What are they? Where am I? Did I pass out?

"Mr. Valvano! James!" It was a male doctor—it had to be Doctor

13

Swartz. His voice was sharp and blunt, and it rudely interrupted the hallucination. I was back in the hospital bed, looking up at him.

I will never forget that morning. I will never forget the first time I heard her voice—the woman named Jade.

January 26, 2009
Monday—9:09 PM

I opened my eyes several minutes ago. I was jolted awake by a strange dream. They were here. They were standing at the foot of my bed. I know they were. Thanks to poor vision, and a wicked high from whatever drugs they are supplying, I could not make out their faces. I remember looking up at them, and for several seconds they remained there—motionless—like five lifeless ice burgs. I was not afraid of them. Strangely, I felt like I knew them. In their presence, I felt secure and guarded. Still, I had no idea who they were. I knew they were looking down at me, so I waited with anticipation. In tandem, almost like marionettes, they raised their left hands and pointed to the window. I saw the transformation. Downward, a gel-like substance began to fill the window frame until it completely overtook its shape. It remained a wavy, milky shade of grey for several seconds, before it retransformed. The five faceless guests continued to point toward the substance from within the window. Their heads were turned toward it and their outstretched arms remained fixed. The gel began to clear and I struggled hard to see. Gradually I saw the ocean, and into view came an old, relic-like sailboat. Her voice entered the bedroom. It was the woman named Jade. The dark and erroneous guests slowly dropped their arms to their sides. They mechanically, in synchronicity, turned toward me, and I followed their slow and methodical movements.

This was you…before…

I listened to her voice and turned once again to view the gel-filled window.

FLASH

Everything was up close and bright. My eyes were new eyes. Clearly, I saw the man, but it was not me.

Look again James.

The man was dressed in white linen, and around his right wrist was a golden band of some sort. Around his neck, he wore a tight gold choker, and hanging from its center was a green stone the size of a half dollar piece. The sun afforded both pieces of jewelry just enough light to shimmer and gleam as the boat continued its unknown course. He was at the helm of the vessel, and his shoulder-length, dirty blonde hair danced wildly in the ocean breeze. His clean-shaven face was strong and his jaw line was well defined. His frame was solid and quite muscular. This lone traveler was definitely not me.

Look deeper James…deeper.

***

As I heard her voice, the man looked directly at me. His eyes met mine and a flash of white filled the room. I remained blinded by the light for mere seconds, and then I saw once again. The boat was old. It was nothing I had ever seen before. The view of the ocean was wide and long; a landmass of any kind was nowhere to be found. I felt the sea breeze against my face and the jewelry against my skin. My body was powerfully built, and I could feel the linen fabric upon my skin. I felt his muscles—my muscles flex and contract, as I held the boat's wheel tightly in my hands. I felt everything, even hair blowing against my face freely in the wind. It was his hair and his face. It was my hair and my face. It was our hair and our face. We, indeed, were one in the same. Another thing was for sure. I was at the helm of this old ship without any concept of direction or destination.

It is not time, James.

I heard Jade's voice again, and in the path of my boat, something began to rise from the water. It was directly ahead, and it was colossal. It was as if a Blue Whale opened its mouth at the surface of the water, but it was more mechanical—more structural and metallic. It continued to rise upward, and the boat maintained its course toward the structure. It felt like being on the lift hill of a massive rollercoaster, with just seconds to spare before falling downward into its steel bowels.

You are not ready to see. You must look from within. Then and only then will you be able to see with your eyes.

FLASH

Once the white light cleared, I was in total darkness. The boat rocked to one side and back again. A second later, it happened once more, but this time my relic craft capsized. I was fighting among the waves within the darkness.

You will know when it is time, James.

FLASH

Jade's voice resonated within my head, just as the white light penetrated my eyes. My body was drawn backward; I felt it being pulled viciously. Then the mattress was against my back. I was returned to my room, inside my own body, on top of my bed. I opened my eyes. It was dark, calm and so very lonely. I peered over to my vacant window. There was no boat, nor was there an image of my former self. There was nothing but shadows of whatever lingered outside in the night. I will sit here for a little while longer. I have to hold on and wait. More importantly, I must hope that everything will make sense. Am I going crazy? Am I already there?

January 29, 2009
Thursday—10:36PM

The first words I heard today were—Good morning. The voice was recognizable and warm. I began to wake from a fog and turned to see my partner, Ian.

Ian dragged the hospital chair closer to the bed. I suddenly noticed the absence of the tubes, and the irritating sensation from my groin was gone.

Thank God, they removed the catheter!

I peered to my left and the machine was still there, standing beside my bed. Some random wiring came down from the mechanism and made its way to the left side of my head, just above my ear.

What the hell is going on? Was the accident that bad?

"Hey you, it's time to wake up." Ian spoke, trying to gain my attention.

I looked over at him and our eyes met. Everything was still blurry, but I could see that he was smiling at me. He had also been crying. He took my right hand in his, and the result of his touch was both soothing and painful.

"I knew you'd come back. You've been in and out of sleep for just over a week." I could tell from his shaky voice that he was worried and worn.

Come back. Where the hell am I? I have so many questions!

Ian's facial expression changed. He could sense the absolute frustration exuding from within me. I gripped his hand, and struggled to get the words out.

"Ian what happened?" It felt like sandpaper had been jammed down my throat.

"Give me a second." Ian replied. "I'll be right back."

Ian let go of my hand and suddenly vanished behind the curtain. A second later, I heard the door close behind him.

What is he up to?

I needed my eyeglasses. I looked down at my body, scanning every facet of my frame. I had to make sure everything was still there, attached, and working. I wiggled my toes; there was pain. I moved my feet; there was pain. I moved my arms, hands, and fingers; there was pain.

Everything is working. I need my eyeglasses!

I noticed the nodes on my chest and found the wires leading up to the machine. I slowly moved my left hand up to my head and touched the foreign object fixed to my scalp.

What is going on?

I turned my head as far as I could and noticed a nightstand. Peripherally, I glanced at a small clock, and a standard hospital lamp. I slowly reached out to search the nightstand for my eyeglasses. The door open and I heard the unmistakable sound of Ian's footsteps. He came to my bed as I turned to look at him.

"Ian, everything is blurry." My voice was still raw and scratchy.

Ian did not hesitate. He walked around the bed and opened the top draw of the nightstand. I looked up at him and he began to hand them to me, but instead, he placed my eyeglasses on my face.

"Voila…" Ian joked, "No more blurriness."

I panned the room and my eyes confirmed that I was in a hospital. As Ian began to sit, he pulled the chair even closer to my side. He noticed I was taking everything in.

"Can you please adjust the bed so I can sit up?" I asked pointing at the controller snaked around the silver railing.

Ian leaned in, grabbed the unit, and soon the back of the bed was rising.

"Is that better?" Ian asked, as he touched my right hand. I just nodded and conjured a diminutive smile.

"I asked the nurse to call the doctor. He should be here soon. Don't worry about talking right now."

Ian often played 'protector'; however, I noticed how pensive he was. Ian had so much to say, ironically, he was not always the best communicator. In no way was he antisocial, however, quite the reserved conversationalist. His voice was never this uneasy, and masked. I witnessed the challenge in his eyes. He knew me like the back of his hand. Ian became accustomed to being with an Italian who loved to talk, and without notice, I would go off on multiple tangents. However, at that very moment, I could tell that Ian was hoping I would not say a word.

"They will probably take the IV out soon." Ian sounded very assured.

I was listening to his voice, but something so unsettling caught my eyes. I glanced over his shoulder and looked outside the window.

Am I dreaming? This is not possible! This does not happen in Central Florida!

"Are you okay…James?" Ian questioned. He knew I saw it.

Jerk…Jerk…Tick

My body began its daily abnormal movements. I looked straight into his eyes. It took everything I had, and I fought with a moment of dizzying uncertainty.

"I will be fine once you tell me why the hell it's snowing in Florida!" I beamed.

Before Ian could reply, the door opened and someone quickly peeled the privacy drape to one side, exposing Ian and me completely. It was a doctor.

"James, how are you feeling? My name is Doctor Swartz."

I knew who he was. I remembered his voice. I gave him a nod and looked back at Ian. I was waiting for an answer. I was waiting to comprehend everything. I wanted to know what was going on.

"I am the Chief Neurologist here at CNS. We are all very pleased that you are awake. I am going to run additional tests…"

I cut him off—"What is CNS? Where am I, and would someone care to explain the blizzard outside my window?"

The doctor glanced at Ian and then back at me. "CNS stands for Center for Neurological Studies. You have been here with us for some time." He continued to explained, however he was not doing it fast enough.

I cut him off again. "What about the snow!" They both felt uneasy with my outburst. "And, how long have I been here?"

Doctor Swartz took a moment, gave Ian another glance, then his eyes returned to mine.

"James, you have been here just over a year. You suffer from a degenerative neurological disease. You are here because you had an accident, and everyone here at the facility is pleased that you are awake." Doctor Swartz was holding back, and I could not deal with it.

"Doctor, I know. I remember the day I went to get the test results. I remember the car accident. Why does my body hurt so badly?" The monitor began to 'beep' faster. They both saw my anger brewing.

The Doctor turned toward Ian and gave him that 'look' once again. "James, we will do everything possible to make sure you are comfortable. The fatigue you are experiencing is due to atrophy. Like I said, you have been in a coma for a long time, and now we must help you regain full function of your extremities."

A nurse entered the room and interrupted him. "Doctor, is everything okay?"

"Actually, have someone take Mr. Valvano for a complete evaluation, MRI, and blood work." Doctor Swartz gave the nurse verbal orders while he quickly jotted a note on a small white pad. "And, please get this to Doctor O'Shea." He tore the note from the pad and handed it to the nurse. She turned and left the room.

I looked at Ian. "I am confused. Where are we?"

This time Ian turned and looked at the doctor. It seemed as if Ian was asking for permission without saying a word. Doctor Swartz gave him a quick nod.

"James, take things slowly, and I will see you soon." Doctor Swartz tried his best to be cordial. He quickly left the room.

Ian didn't give me a chance to speak again. He took this time to explain. "When you had your accident you suffered a severe head injury. We rushed to the hospital. That same night you slipped into a coma, and they told us that you would probably never recover. The whole family was devastated. The doctors all agreed that it was unfortunate. Not only were you diagnosed with a degenerative brain disease, but now a head injury."

Tick...Jerk...Jerk

I listened closely to what Ian was telling me. I felt the pain in his words, but he knew I had more questions, and I most definitely needed answers.

"Ian how did I get here and has it really been over a year?"

Ian sat back in the chair and folded his hands. "I know you have many questions and I will tell you everything." Ian paused. "You just woke up for the second time and I want to make sure you are going to stay awake. You need to take it easy and let them run all the tests they need to."

"Second time?" I was perplexed. What else am I going to find out?

"You had been here from about three months. One afternoon a nurse came in to check on you, and noticed that you were awake. She said that you were whispering something, however the nurse had difficulty understanding you. About ten minutes later, you fell back into a coma. We were so hopeful, and I never gave up on you." I saw the pain in Ian's eyes.

***

Remember it James...Remember...

Ian was still talking, but his words began to fade into the background. I heard her voice inside my head. It was Jade. Without warning, a discharge of white light hit my eyes. I was blinded, and then a second later, I saw myself beneath the blue water. I saw her hands. I searched for her face. I wanted to reach out to touch her, but her hands directed me downward. I witnessed thousands of sea creatures, as they swam within the ocean's vastness. The colors were amazing, as was the breathtaking view. I remember the emotions and my desire to swim among them—all of them. I remember searching for my seal, and for Jade. My eyes consumed the magnitude of the deep, and my ears began to catch the sound of the whales...

Focus... You must listen to your heart... Listen, and everything will become clear...

"James! Are you okay?" Ian's voice brought me back. Another bright flare hit my eyes, and then I saw him. "Are you okay?"

Tick...Tick...Jerk

"I am fine." I felt beads of sweat trailing down from my brow. I didn't know how to explain it to Ian, and at that moment, I didn't know if I should. "Ian, just tell me how I got here?" I wiped my forehead and decided to steer away from the previous interruption. Ian moved in closer and took my hand.

"Do you remember what we went through just for you to receive Social Security, and Medicaid?" He questioned.

I remembered. How could anyone forget? The process was quite simple, but what happened afterward was a nightmare. Just after the diagnosis, I applied for Social Security, then medical assistance. I started receiving SSI, and we were so pleased that Medicaid kicked in soon after. Nevertheless, bureaucracy stepped up to the plate. Just as quickly as they gave me medical coverage, the State of Florida took it away! We were left to pay for everything! Out of pocket, we were out of luck! I was told that I would have to wait twenty-four months before receiving medical coverage. It didn't matter to *them*. Had I been the mother of five children and had the luxury of driving one of my baby-daddy's BMW's, things would have worked out nicely for me.

"Yes Ian, I remember what we went through." I replied.

"Well, when you had the accident, a specialist gave us the names of five facilities. These institutions willingly accept patients without any costs involved." Ian paused for a moment. "And you know our financial situation…"

I saw that Ian was in such pain. His eyes began to water, and I continued to let him speak.

"I had to make the decision to transfer you here. This facility is well equipped to handle your disease. They are a research institute and a hospital combined. They complete trial studies and work with geneticists, and many other specialists."

He didn't have to take you away from Florida!

"You know I hate the snow!" I exclaimed. I couldn't control it.

"Please James, not now." Ian snapped. "Can't you see this is already difficult for me?"

We stared at each other for several seconds. Grilling him on the weather was the last thing he deserved or needed at this state of the game.

Jerk…Tick…Tick

"I'm sorry Ian. I am just so confused and…" I tried to apologize, but Ian put one finger on my lips.

"Everything will be okay, just let the doctors do what they can." Tears fell from his eyes. At that very moment, it became clear to me. I realized he went through hell while I was in the coma. We sat there together in silence just looking at each other. I could not fathom what he experienced all these months. I knew if the tables were turned, I would have been an absolute basket case. Living without Ian would be like living without air—impossible. I broke a smile and told him that I loved him. Ian was not the type of person to show emotion easily. He was usually solid, and internalized everything, but today he let the flood gates open.

"Excuse me." Nurse Clemins moaned, as she knocked on the door and entered the room at the same time. "We have to run some tests." She had great timing and such couth. Without reserve, I knew I was not going to like this woman!

Ian stood up and wiped away his tears. He had to get back into form. The ex-Brit had to regain his composure.

"Honey, I need you to take this." Nurse Clemins had a medicine cup in her hand, and before I could say a word, she emptied the contents of the cup into my mouth. Ian quickly reached over to the bedside stand and provided a small cup of water.

"Angela," Ian began, "What exactly did the doctor say?" He noticed I was becoming edgy. It became obvious to me that I had been here for as long as they said. Ian and the nurse were on a first name basis.

"Another medication regimen will begin tomorrow, following James' visit with Doctor O'Shea." As Nurse Clemins informed us, she began to remove the nodes from my chest, including the one on the left side of my head.

"What did you just give him?" Ian asked.

"Gosh, I'm sorry. It's a sedative," Nurse Clemins looked at me. "You'll be better off sedated while having the MRI. It can be a bit claustrophobic inside the tunnel."

Jerk...Tick...Tick

"Hold still honey." She began to remove the intravenous from my left arm. I cringed. Ian knew I hated needles, and given the choice, I would rather have my head run over by a locomotive.

"Okay honey, that's it." The nurse recognized my discomfort.

"When is he going to have the MRI?" Ian asked.

"Frank will be here in about twenty-five minutes to escort James. Let's give the sedative a chance to work." She responded.

Nurse Clemins smiled and left the room. She tried to be pleasant, but it wouldn't have mattered what she did. I did not like her. I looked up at Ian and he looked tired, so tired.

"Just relax, and let the sedative work." Ian placed his hand on my head and I closed my eyes.

Thoughts began to build, and moments later, a gentle white light sucked me in. I stood in the sand listening to the waves. The water crept to my feet and receded back again. I felt myself wanting to stay there. I wanted to feel safe and held. An unknown force would not allow me to enter the water beyond my ankles. I continued to look out into the ocean and heard her voice calling my name. Her voice was so compelling. Although I saw her only once, I had the feeling we had known each other before. Somehow, we too, were connected. The tears began to fall from my eyes. All I wanted was to venture back to that special place. Then I heard the ocean begin to cry. I experienced its sadness and the mutual need we had for each other was physically powerful, and emotionally riveting. I scanned the beach but it was completely vacant. I was alone…standing alone…wishing I could return to the sea.

You are not ready yet, James…Search for the strength within yourself…

The beach went silent, and everything suddenly froze. The water, the seagulls, the air, remained still and lifeless. It was then that I noticed a light begin to build. It began to emerge from within the water.

"James," Ian whispered, and I opened my eyes, "Frank is here."

Please no, I want to go back! I need to go back!

"Hi James, I am Frank. I am going to take you for your MRI. Your body has suffered a bit from degeneration, so you'll feel weak and there may be some discomfort."

Frank was very careful and within seconds, I was out of the bed, and into the wheelchair.

I looked at Ian, and he tried to make me relax. "I'll be here James, don't stress."

Frank was at least my age, and medium build. He fit the typical blue-eyed blonde hair stereotype. He mumbled a few words while wheeling me down the hallway, but I was too busy looking at the different rooms as we moved along. We passed by a room filled with workout machines—obviously a gym. I felt enclosed in a bubble as the sedative continued to set in. The wheelchair ride took forever, and we passed by another room filled with tables, chairs, and food trays—obviously the cafeteria. I closed my eyes and felt Frank guide the wheelchair. I failed to notice that we entered the elevator until I opened my eyes again to see the doors close. The lift took us down a level, and opened into a long corridor. Frank was on the move and we snaked quickly through the hallways, until we came to a large white door.

Imaging Center
Room 17B Access

Frank whipped out a white plastic card, swiped it, and then entered his code onto the small display. In seconds, the white door slid open and we entered a dimly lit room. I continued to feel the hold of the sedative. I scanned the room and noticed the huge mechanism.

Tick…Tick…Jerk

"I need to take your eyeglasses." Frank said, removing them from my face. He noticed the sedative had further set in. It was hard for me to keep my eyes open, and my head from bobbing. Moments later a woman entered through another door from within the room.

***

"Thanks Frank, let's get James on the table and I'll take it from here."

I could feel both of them help me out of the chair, but my eyes were fixed on the long table. It began to slide out from within the tunnel. It came to a stop, and both Frank and the technician positioned my body on it.

"James, I am Cindy. I'm going to give you a few instructions and then I will be behind that window monitoring you." The technician began adjusting the machine, as I looked up at her.

I didn't notice, but Frank was already leaving the room. He gave her a wave and exited the room.

Cindy raised her voice, "Frank I will page you to escort James back to his room."

I heard the door close with a 'hiss'—Frank was gone.

Cindy placed some type of helmet gear on my head. I was drifting. I was fading fast.

Jerk…Tick

"We have to make sure that you do not move during the process."

27

Cindy instructed as she strapped my right arm and right leg down with Velcro restraints. "Don't worry."

It was evident why the right side of my body needed restraints. I used to joke with family and friends. I used to tell them not to stand so close unless they wanted a black eye or a bruised arm.

"You may hear thumping or clanging sounds, but don't be startled." Cindy warned.

The sedative began to take me deeper. As she continued to speak, I felt the pull of the poison. Cindy looked down at me and pointed behind her shoulder, "I'll be right out there. You will be fine. Just close your eyes and take a nap."

I was slowly drowning…fading. Moments later the table was gradually moving backward. Under the thick relentless cloud of poison, the moment took me back to a cartoon. I was the Damsel in distress, strapped down on a conveyer belt with moments left to spare before being mauled by a giant saw. I took the Tech's advice. I closed my eyes and headed into the belly of the magnetic beast.

I drifted…slowly…peacefully…

FLASH

I was at the water's edge, and again, all sound was gone. Something was wrong. The sun was shining down on my skin, but I could not feel its warmth. I was standing in the sand; however, I could not feel its gritty texture beneath my feet. I called out to the expanse; however, my own voice was absent. The waves rolled in and passed over my feet, and again I felt nothing. Seagulls flew above me, minus the sound of their squawking. I tried to move toward the water. I wanted to swim…swim as far as I could…as deep as I could…I needed the ocean to hold me again. I needed to see my seal again. I needed to understand. I had to understand.

You are not ready. You will know the time.

It was Jade. Her voice punctured the silence. It almost felt as if my insides were being ripped forward, out of my body—de-shelled.

Suddenly, I could feel the sand beneath my feet. I could hear the waves crashing and feel the rushing water overtake over my feet. I could feel the sun beating down on my skin. She stood behind me, but I did not turn to see her.

You must be able to hear it again. You will know when it is time.

The deafening silence slammed back down onto the beach. The inability for me to feel anything—the sun on my skin, the sand, and water at my feet, vanished.

Please tell me what is happening. Please help me understand.

You must find it yourself. Once you do, you will be free.

I don't understand. Why is this happening to me?

Find it deep within yourself. No one can show you. It is here, but only you can find the way.

"James, we are done. You did a great job." I was on the table, looking up at Cindy. She held the controller in her hand. Her voice broke me from my encounter.

"Are you feeling okay?" she asked.

Still groggy, I looked up at her and nodded. I heard the door open and Frank entered with the wheelchair. Cindy removed the Velcro straps, then the helmet. Frank helped me off the padded table back into the chair. The sedative was obviously still in play, and I only felt mild discomfort.

"Alright James," Frank began, "I'll take you back to your room so you can rest."

***

Frank already had me wheeled halfway down the hallway. The maze of left and right turns was awaiting us, but deep inside my mind, I was back at the beach. I was overtaken by the power of these visions…dreams…reveries.

"Tomorrow morning you have an appointment with Doctor O'Shea." Frank advised under a few heavy breaths. "So get a good night's sleep tonight, and I'll be there after breakfast tomorrow morning."

Jade. What is going on?

January 30, 2009
Friday 9:55PM

This morning the nurse came to remove my breakfast tray, and Frank was at my bedside, wheelchair in tow. Although I could not build a connection with any of the other nurses, Frank was able to understand me. He was different. He helped me out of bed and offered some small talk. I was too busy griping about the weather, and the snow, and did not realize we were already at the elevator. The door opened and off came two nurses. They smiled and wished us a good morning. We entered the elevator and Frank pressed the button for the third floor. He began to hum a tune while I sat preoccupied.

Who is Doctor O'Shea?

The elevator door opened to a nurse's station. One nurse was on the phone and the other one gave us a wave.

"Good morning Mr. Valvano, I'm Clara. It's nice to see you."

I waved back, but Frank continued to wheel me past the station, then into an undersized hallway.

"Nurse Clara is a hoot, but the other one is menopausal." Frank thought I should know.

Jerk…Tick…Tick

We soon entered a beautiful, parlor-like room. This was unlike any doctor's office I had ever seen. There was a gas fireplace flickering in the center of the room, and a huge picture window with an excellent view of the courtyard below. I asked Frank to wheel me over to the window, and he did. I noticed that it snowed again last night. Snow powdered all the trees, benches, and pathways. Frank gave me a moment to look outside then wheeled me back around to the desk. To the far side of the window sat a chocolaty brown, chaise lounge. Various abstract paintings covered the entire wall, opposite the window.

"Are those Jackson Pollock's?" I pointed at two paintings, which hung side-by-side.

Frank didn't know who the artist was. He continued to wheel me in front of an elegant cherry desk. The expensive piece of furniture stood on a long area rug, suffused in multiple earth tones. The space was amazingly warm and tastefully decorated.

Then, it hit my eyes, and it registered clearly.

A phone!

It was there, it was real, but most of all it screamed freedom. It screamed—connection! It bellowed—pick me up! It sat straight in front of me. It was resting on the desk bating me. I was waiting for this moment! Once Frank leaves, I can call anyone—someone.

Jerk…Tick…Tick…

Frank noticed how transfixed I was on the phone. I tried not to be so palpable, so I looked up behind the desk.

Leave! Hurry up and leave…

Built into the wall was a spacious, ornate shelving unit. On each of the shelves, several pictures, trinkets, and books, sat perfectly.

"Okay James." Frank began. "Doctor O'Shea should be right in. I will come to get you in a bit." Frank turned around and left the room. He also left the door opened.

If I do it quickly, I can at least make one call!

I tried to distract myself by continuing to observe the room. I tried to control my heartbeat, and the urge to make a call. There was a filing cabinet to the left side of the desk. I looked back at the shelving unit and noticed all of the pictures were of scenery; there were fields of sunflowers, tulips, hills of green, and streams of water.

Make the call! Make any Call!

Moments later, I heard the sound of heals heading closer to the door. In walked a tall, brown-haired woman dressed quite nicely. She wore a dark blue blouse and black slacks. She looked at me and smiled.

Jerk...Tick...

"Good morning James, I am sorry for the wait." She apologized.

Instinctively, yet robotically, she moved behind her desk, placed her briefcase down, and then proceeded to the coat rack.

You cannot call yourself a doctor without the long white coat!

After she put it on, she sat down and pulled out a white-pad, a pen, and a folder.

"How are you doing this morning James? My name is Doctor O'Shea."

"I guess I am fine. Are we here to discuss the results of the MRI? I'd like Ian to be here too?" I presumed.

Doctor O'Shea revealed a smile and informed me that she was not at all a radiologist, but a psychiatrist. She noticed the change of expression on my face.

"Do not become alarmed." She began speaking in a soft and calm manner. "Each patient here at CNS visits with me at least once a week. I am here to help you adjust. You just recently woke after being in a coma for over a year, but most importantly, I wish to help you process aspects of your condition."

Tick...Tick...Jerk...

Cross your arms! Don't let her see!

I was not embarrassed nor did I feel nervous. I had seen a few therapists in Florida, and never felt ashamed to admit it. However, I was taken by surprise and did not expect to see one today. It would have been nice had I been presented with the option.

"It is important for us to get to know one another." She outlined. "I want you to feel comfortable, however if you experience any fatigue, I'll have Frank escort you back to your room."

Doctor O'Shea seemed decent, however I knew all about the psychological babble.

"So tell me how you are feeling." She pressed ahead with the obvious and magical first question. It was the question of all questions. It was what I considered, the proverbial cement, which begins the bonding process between Doctor and Patient.

It took me a moment to gather my thoughts, and to maintain a straight face. "I wasn't prepared to see a therapist today."

Doctor O'Shea did not reply. She continued to look at me—studying me.

"Don't get me wrong, I am not uncomfortable with therapy." I reworded my previous statement. "I just wish someone would have told me that we were going to meet today."

"I understand." She replied. "I apologize for the miscommunication. Would you like to reschedule our appointment, or just wait until you are ready?" Doctor O'Shea was trying her best to be hospitable, but an undertone of sarcasm was easily identifiable.

"No, we can talk today. Why put it off." If not today, we'd have to meet another time, so putting it off would have been counterintuitive.

Doctor O'Shea began to prepare herself. She took the cap off her designer pen. "Okay then. So, how are you feeling?" She looked down at her white pad and waited. "Feel free to start anywhere you'd like."

Jerk...Jerk...Tick

"Well, I'm a bit frustrated. It's hard to accept that I was in a coma for so long. I hate that I have to rely on a wheelchair."

I stopped and waited for her. The entire situation was odd.

"Go on. I want you to just speak your mind and we'll take it from there." She peered up at me and waited again.

"I often feel frustrated and sometime disoriented. I've been thinking about the accident. I remember the day I received the test results and I know that I crashed my car, but I have no recollection of anything after that. Actually, all the pieces seem to blur."

Doctor O'Shea looked up from her pad. "After what you experienced, I can understand." She paused. "You mentioned frustration and disorientation?"

I began to feel beads of sweat build on my brow, and my back began to feel wet.

Jerk…Jerk…Tick

I sat there looking at the phone. She slowly tapped her pen against the desk. The sound began to build steadily and continued to work on my last nerve. I wanted to lunge across the desk and break the pen in half!

"James, please go on. What makes you frustrated? " Her voice was irritatingly sharp.

Stop with the damned pen!

"Isn't it obvious?" I barked. The pen tapping stopped and I looked directly into her eyes. "I woke up in a hospital bed in a different state, with snow outside my window. I had tubes down my throat, an IV in my arm, and a catheter in my penis. There were probes of all kind attached to my body, and then I was told I had been in a coma for over a year. So, if you need to know why I am frustrated, then there you have it!"

Tick…Jerk…Tick…

The doctor paused for a moment then wrote a few notes. "Yes, you have been through quite a bit. I can appreciate your forwardness." She continued to look down at her notes, but I caught the awkward grin on her face. "Ian told me that you were the type of person who gets right to the point and does not mix words."

I did not reply to her comment. That much was true. I was not the type to beat around the bush, and it bothered me whenever someone would. However, what was more important was the phone, which sat just over a foot away from me.

I wish I had my cell phone. Ian will give me his cell phone.

"James, I want you to know that I am here to help." She was looking at me, but I did not look up at her. "I can help you understand your neurological disease, and what the future holds."

Without hesitation, she opened the folder. There were a few moments of silence as she fingered through page after page, scanning its contents.

Tick…Jerk…

"I've reviewed your medical history for the last ten years. You were treated for depression and anxiety for most of that period." She cut to the chase.

Prozac—Paxel—Wellbutrin—None of them did anything but cause a seventy-five pound weight gain!

"Ian specified that you voluntarily sought therapy, is that correct?" I knew from her voice that she was now getting down to business.

Tick…Tick…Jerk

"Do you doubt Ian?" I interjected, this time I looked up at her.

Doctor O'Shea said nothing, but continued to look at me.

I continued. "Yes, I did choose to get therapy and the most wonderful thing happened."

The doctor raised her eyebrows and waited for my response.

"After seeing the fifth therapist, I noticed that I had less money in my bank account and heard everything I already knew."

Doctor O'Shea definitely was a gambler, or at least she learned how to put on an exceptional, bulletproof, poker face.

"So, what are you saying James? Did these professionals fail you, or did they help you find the answers you needed?" She refused to let up. "It seems quite peculiar that you continued to seek the insight of five therapists, yet you already had all the answers." She never loosened her unremitting stare.

I regrouped, and decided to try this from another angle—the truth. "Doctor O'Shea, for the longest time I knew there was something wrong with me. I never understood why I was always depressed. I battled anxiety and moodiness for many years. I never wanted to be in large groups, and I dreaded social engagements. None of the therapists knew what was truly wrong with me, so I continued to take the prescribed antidepressants. I kept my family in the dark for a long time, and only turned to Ian."

Tick…Jerk…

Doctor O'Shea spoke. "From what I have seen and heard, you truly do have a fabulous safety net. I've had the pleasure of meeting some of your friends and family while you were in the coma. I've actually had most of them here in this very room, and they all understand the sensitivity of your condition."

She saw the change in my eyes and posture.

"James, does it surprise you that they came to visit?" she asked.

"No, not at all," I felt my heart race. "Do they know I am awake? Are they coming?" She saw me glare at the phone once again.

Tick…Tick…Jerk…

"Yes, your family is aware." Doctor O'Shea replied. "However, it is imperative that we take things gradually before introducing outside stimuli." She chose her words carefully. "Your brother John is still living in a group home in Orlando. Sadly, your parents informed us that the disease has progressed. He is now suffering from dementia, and they are dealing with quite a bit right now."

She paused for a few moments, took a couple of notes, and then began to speak. "Your family and friends have had no choice but to accept the outcome of this disease. They are troubled, nevertheless they understand it is a terminal disease, and they are doing the best they can to cope. They know that we are here to provide the best possible treatment for you." Doctor O'Shea looked back on her notes.

"James, Ian said that you went to get tested soon after your brother John was diagnosed. Can you tell me why you acted so quickly?" She was still searching through her notes.

"Well, it's not that difficult to explain. I knew deep inside that going to the doctor and having blood drawn was just a procedure. I already diagnosed myself. Over a period of ten years, I experienced jerking in my right arm and right leg. As I said, I dealt with depression and anxiety. I knew I had the disease." I stopped and waited for her to look up at me.

"Go on." She requested. She continued to write.

"Well, based on what I researched and the fact that I was showing symptoms, seemed enough for me. None of us would have known had John not been diagnosed. Actually, I would have been surprised if my test results came back negative."

Tick…Tick…Tick

She finally looked up at me, but seemed confused. "What about the day you saw Doctor Spinzer, and the accident? You had already diagnosed yourself, yet you were shocked when he gave you the results."

"Maybe I reacted that way because it was official." I replied.

"Validated?" She threw back at me.

Tick...Tick...

"I guess so." I volleyed.

She hit a nerve and made me think back to the accident. My hands suddenly started to sweat and I felt antsy. I could almost feel my hands on the steering wheel. Dr. Spinzer's voice reverberated within my head.

Mr. Valvano...I'm sorry...It's terminal...

I saw the minivan full of balloons. Then, like a scratched album, my memory skipped, and I could feel the car flip repeatedly. Splintered pieces of glass hit my face, but there was silence. It was as if an old movie was playing without sound. I saw nothing other than the road, then the sky.

Tick...Jerk

"What are you thinking about James?" She prodded.

I looked at her and took a deep breath. I wanted so badly to remember everything...every single moment of the incident. It bothered me! I was unable to recall what happened that day. Will I ever know? Am I going crazy?

Jerk...Jerk...Tick

"James?" She was persistent, and quickly got my attention.

"Well, it's obvious. I shouldn't have been behind the wheel! I made a big mistake to drive that day, and now I am paying for that decision. Going alone to receive the test results was stupid. If I did things differently, I wouldn't be here with a year of my life gone!" I wanted to get up and run. I wanted my body back! She was not helping!

Tick...Tick...Jerk

She continued to press my buttons. "Can you tell me about the accident? Can you remember specific details? Can you recall anything?"

Tick...Tick

I tried to calm down and answer her questions, but there was no way out of it. Any chance of a rapid escape from this conversation was futile. My heart raced steadily.

I replayed what I could remember. "I recall Doctor Spinzer giving me the results. I remember walking out of the building. I do not remember getting into my vehicle, or even starting it up. I know there are pieces missing!"

Shut her up!

"I pulled out of the driveway and I remember there were two cars ahead of me." I paused and tried to make myself remember, but nothing would come. I became so uncomfortable and I wanted to leave her office! My body was sweating and I felt overwhelmingly hot.

"Go on, take your time." She insisted. She kept pushing.

Jerk…Jerk…Tick

"I remember the two cars ahead of me…they turned right, but that's where it ends. I only remember feeling the car tumble and glass on my face, but I don't know what I hit, or what hit me!" A moment of reality and panic came over me. "I don't even know if I hurt or killed anyone!"

Tick…Tick…Jerk

Doctor O'Shea broke in. "You didn't hurt anyone…just relax." Her voice was concerning.

I felt myself wanting to hit or throw something. "I hate the fact that I am here, and not home in Florida. I had twenty-one years of that crap." I pointed toward the window and the falling snow outside. "Ian knows I hate the cold weather and the goddamned snow."

Doctor O'Shea took another note. "Do you want to receive the necessary treatment and get back to your life, or not?" She dared to ask.

Control yourself. Keep your arms crossed! She needs to shut her mouth!

The room was closing in on me. Claustrophobia was winning and about to take my last breath.

"Well of course I do!" I shouted. "I want to walk again and get the hell out of here! I want my life back!"

Tick…Tick…Tick

Doctor O'Shea looked at me. "What else do you want James?" she asked.

"I want to speak with my family and friends!" I was still shouting. "I have no phone in my room, so that's not going to happen. I will not go outside in that weather, so here I am—trapped. And I have no idea where the hell I am!"

Doctor O'Shea stopped writing. She threw her white-pad down in front of her and with both hands, grabbed the phone from the desk, and slammed it down in front of me. "If you think making a call to your parents or anyone else at this time will help, then go right ahead!"

I did not expect her reaction. The phone was right there and I felt myself grabbing it. I wanted to speak to someone…anyone.

"You've been fixated on the phone since I walked in!" She began to raise her voice. "Go ahead, and call your parents who are already going through their own personal hell! Call a friend if you would like. What will that accomplish? How do you think they will respond to your current state of mind?" She was loud and unrelenting.

Tick…Jerk…Tick

"I just want to hear their voices. I want to reconnect." I felt my stomach turn, and my eyes emptied tears of pain and anger.

"Go ahead and call your parents. Tell them how trapped and miserable you are. It doesn't matter what they are going through, right?" Doctor O'Shea beamed.

"I don't want to hurt anyone, especially my mom and dad." I could barely speak. "I miss everyone."

"James, I understand. I really do." She lowered her voice. "Let's make a pact. I want you to complete your physical therapy and get stronger."

I sat in the wheelchair and realized for the first time that I was no longer the navigator of my own life. This was going to kill me, and no one was going to be able to kiss this pain away.

FLASH

The white light hit my eyes, but I remained in the room with the Doctor.

Focus your energy, James.

FLASH

"I want you to take all the necessary medications I prescribe, and attend all scheduled sessions." Doctor O'Shea continued with her demands. "Once you have had ample time to face things head on, I will allow for phone calls and visits."

Tick...Jerk...

Although I still felt the urge to pick up her phone, I realized that I couldn't cause any additional pain for my family. I could not risk hearing my mom cry. Doctor O'Shea reached for the phone and positioned it back at her side.

"I am only here to help you." Her tone was leveling. "I will not lie to you. The road ahead will be tough. If you work hard, I know things will get better."

I didn't have the energy to reply or fight. I felt alone and so angry. She looked at me and stated we were done for today. Doctor O'Shea picked up the phone, pressed two buttons, waited, mumbled something, and then hung it up.

"If you need to see me before next week, just ask any of the nurses to page me." Doctor O'Shea opened her day planner and jotted a note. "We will meet here in my office, every Friday at 10AM."

She stood up, placed the planner in her briefcase, and went to file the folder in the cabinet. She turned and looked at me. "By the way James, thank you."

Jerk...Tick...

I looked at her and did not know what to say. Why was she thanking me? Maybe she was the one who needed the therapy!

"Thank you for the privilege of getting to know you." She added. "We have a way to go, but I know it will be okay."

There was sudden movement at the door.

"Doctor O'Shea." Frank said as he popped his head inside. It was great timing of course. I wanted out!

"Yes Frank, we are finished today." She looked away from him and back at me. "The medication regimen will begin tomorrow morning and the nurses will keep me informed daily."

I nodded. Frank quickly took hold of the wheelchair, and swiftly we made our way toward the elevator.

"Boy, we heard you guys from down the hall. You need to calm down." Frank decided to put in his two cents.

"Go to hell Frank!" I snapped.

"I hate to be the one to tell you, but we are already there." Frank noted.

JACK ASS!

"You have your first physical therapy session tomorrow at 1PM. After lunch I will come get you." Frank declared.

As we faced the nurse's station from inside the elevator, the doors began to close. That is when I heard her voice. It was just before the elevator doors touched.

This place is going to kill you!

January 31, 2009
Saturday 11:09PM

Frank was never late. He arrived at my room this morning on time. It was 8:30AM, and I was happy to be out of the hospital gown and into a pair of socks, sweats, and a T-shirt. As expected, Frank helped me into the wheelchair, and in a flash, he wheeled me down the hall and into the physical therapy room. It was the first time I actually saw other patients. I was preoccupied and restless, and I sized up the room like a hawk. A woman in the back corner saw us coming toward us, and gave a big wave. Frank moved quickly. There were two elderly men lifting tiny dumbbells, and just behind them was an elderly woman riding a stationary bicycle. Then I noticed a younger woman—she had to be close to my age. She was walking on a treadmill and I could see the perspiration on her face and shirt. I sensed something about her; there was something ominous within her. She looked at me as Frank wheeled me further into the room. It only took that one glance. Our eyes met for a single moment and I felt the emptiness within her. She was in pain—emotional pain.

What does she know about pain?

"James, this is Tonya." Frank introduced us, but I was too caught up in *her*. "She is the head of our Physical Therapy department."

I finally looked up at the woman Frank was introducing. She was a tall woman with short dirty-brown hair—a plain Jane.

"Hi James, how are you feeling today?" Tonya was very hyperactive and reminded me of an overly excited cheerleader.

Jerk...Tick...

"I'm doing okay." I replied.

"That's great!" She popped. "If you could wheel James over to this table I'd appreciate it Frank."

Frank did as she requested. Out of the chair, and up onto the table I went.

"Thanks Frank, we'll be finished in about thirty minutes." Tonya noted.

Frank said something to her but I was not paying attention. I had already turned my head to see Ian standing in front of the large window outside the therapy room. He smiled and pointed back toward the direction of my room. I nodded and was happy to know that he was here. He waved and left the window.

"Okay James, we are going to work on some range of motion today, and if you experience any pain just let me know." She was too bubbly.

I turned, looked up at her, and grinned. I wanted to regain the use of my body. It was the first step to leaving this place.

February 4, 2009
Wednesday 11:39PM

Who am I? What am I? Where am I? Why is this happening to me? What did I do to deserve this? Why won't my family and friends visit me? Why have they abandoned me? Why can't I just die? Who is going to love me like this?   They are ashamed of me. Everyone I know has left me to die! I am here and they won't visit. They stay away. They choose to stay away.

She makes them stay away! She does!

Each day I peer down at them from this solitary cage. I will never forgive the people outside my window! They know I see them, but they continue to act as if I am not here. I bang on the window as they pass. They hear me. Some of them look up at me, and then quickly turn away. They look away from me—the dirty little secret on the second floor! The others ignore my cries. I beg for their attention…for their help. However, they continue to walk to their cars and go home to their families, to their friends, and to their own clandestine lives. They ignore me. They ignore my existence…my puny and insignificant existence.

God I am scared. I know I will die from this. I am just so scared. I didn't ask for any of this, but somehow I am being punished—trapped—held—imprisoned—shut out—shut in—forgotten—thrown away. When I die, will they even care? Will anyone let them know? Maybe I am already dead to all of them.

James, you are not alone. I will never let anything happen to you…

The Silent Scream

You! Yes, you!
You were there all along, but now you decided to show me your face.
Deep inside all the rage—within my head you nestled in place.
One day you will be found—sought out—yes, little devil—you will pay.
…for everything you made me feel…oh, you will have your day.
Seize the moment my horrific friend, and take all of me while I wait.
Time is your enemy—my friend—the very bitter part of me I hate.
You…Yes, you! The slithering snake—all you do it take!
All the tears, and the confusion…You only wish to destroy the rest of me.
I will let you go without a thought…soon I will be set free.

February 6, 2009
Friday 10:33PM

I sat in front of her this morning. I cannot remember when I woke, what I ate, or who bathed and dressed me. However, I sat in front of her—the all-powerful Doctor O'Shea. I listened to the sound of her voice, but comprehended very little. I was drugged. I was paralyzed by the poison she prescribed. If my body had jerked or ticked, I couldn't recall. I didn't notice, because the high was so influential. This brilliant poison loves and cares for me. It is all I have. I longed to see the little white cup!

She's going to cause your death! Death to the sickened lab-rat!

I could barely keep my eyes opened, but Doctor O'Shea's voice continued to fill the room and space around me. I'm not sure how long I sat there, nor do I remember how long she spoke. I felt myself moving. The wheelchair was hovering along, and the last vision I remember was looking up at Frank. We were in the elevator, his face was long, and his eyes were sad.

"I'll talk to Ian…" Frank's voice was there, but I was only able to capture certain words. "The medication…too strong…I'm sorry."

Frank must have placed me into bed. I faded in and out most of the day, looking up at the ceiling. The daylight vanished, moment by moment, each time I opened my eyes. I know Ian was here. I vaguely remember looking up and hearing them. I remember looking up into a blurry pool of people. They were trying to talk to Ian. I believe it was Doctor Swartz and Doctor O'Shea.

Ian was shouting. "…medications!" His voice was there, and then it wasn't. "What the hell…Why is he like this…Fix this!"

I remember looking up at him and he was so livid. I wanted to reach out and beg him for help, but the only energy I had available was to open and close my eyes.

"…he's not functioning…" Ian's voice was sharp, and then the room went silent. Ian was gone, and so was the day.

The night approached and I opened my eyes again. It was darker than before, but enough light entered through the window. I felt something…someone…at the foot of my bed. I waited to gain some strength before attempting to lift my head. I heard something…someone…it was breathing. I waited for the 'thing' to come to my side, but it didn't. It remained at my feet…breathing…watching. I gathered the last bit of energy I had. I lifted my head and looked. The darkened and uninvited figure spoke.

Welcome to CNS!

It was a woman's voice. The voice was sharp, but throaty.

Welcome to hell!

I remember hearing those words, and nothing more. Who was she? Why would she say that? Although the toxins continued to pull on me, I am hoping that Ian comes back. I don't want to be alone tonight. I don't want to be alone, ever.

February 8, 2009
Sunday 11PM

This afternoon, I was angry. I threw a fit at Doctor Swartz, and Doctor O'Shea. Ian backed me up. I wanted to walk again, or at least begin to walk. Both doctors met me in the middle and agreed to push the physical therapy sessions to six o'clock in the evening, before taking my nine o'clock meds. At least then, I would be more alert and able to function during PT. Tonya tried to keep the sessions short and painless, but I wanted her to press on. I pushed myself to the limit. I felt discomfort, but I was determined to get out of that wheelchair. Tonya saw the difference, and told me that she would write it in her report to the doctors. I almost gave Tonya a stroke. She excused herself and left me at the leg machine. She asked me to take a break while she had to use the restroom. When she returned, I had already gotten up and walked over to the parallel bars. Predictably, Tonya came running and began to freak out. She pleaded with me to sit back down in the chair. I gave her a look and told her to leave the gym or come do her job. I began to walk between the bars. She quickly hustled to my side and watched as I took one small step after another. I reached the end of the mat and turned around. She leaned in and placed one hand under my armpit and the other on my forearm. When I accomplished two passes on the parallel bars, I turned to her and she smiled.

49

I did it! I actually did it!

I saw Frank enter the gym. Once he noticed I was standing at the bars, he shook his head and brandished a sly smile. Tonya moved the wheelchair closer to where I stood. I sat down and heard Frank coming from behind.

"Mr. Valvano, should we now call you Superman?" He spouted.

I turned the wheelchair around and glared up at him. "No, you shouldn't, Wonder Woman."

Frank stuck his tongue out at me, and Tonya had a difficult time holding back a laugh. I got used to Frank and his antics and he got used to my sharp Italian tongue. I was comfortable with him, as he was with me.

"Just for that, you shouldn't receive a damn thing." Frank was quite melodramatic. "What do you think Tonya, should I give him the surprise?"

"I'm not getting in the middle of this one." She put her hands up. "I will see you tomorrow James. The two of you are going to drive me to drink!" Tonya patted me on the shoulder and walked away.

"I guess I have no choice but to give you the surprise, although after what you just pulled, I'd give you nothing—nada—zilch." Frank continued to play, while steering the wheelchair.

"Frank, I could care less." I spouted. "All I want is a shower, a bag of pretzels, and you out of my face." I tried to put up a smoke screen. I wanted the flipping surprise!

The gym's automatic doors opened and Frank wheeled me toward the elevator. I kept quiet and pretended not to care about any stupid surprise. After we entered the lift, he looked down and shot me a smirk. The elevator went up and quickly stopped on the second floor. The doors opened to yet another nurse's station. It was dimly lit and quiet.

"Okay, you won! Where are we going?" I gave in.

Before he could say anything, I saw Ian pop his head out of a room far down the hallway. As we continued to move ahead, I noticed that there were several doors on either side of the corridor. When we finally reached Ian, I noticed a small-embossed frame with—Room 201—in white letters. Under the frame was a slot with my full name printed on a white card.

"Welcome to your new room." Ian beamed.

Tick…Tick…

Frank wheeled me in and everything hit me all at once. It looked like a hotel efficiency suite, minus a stove, and microwave oven. As I entered, I noticed the carpet was a deep brown earth tone. A full sized bed sat evenly in the room adorned with an African style comforter.

That's our comforter.

Above the bed hung a gold framed picture of a mother tiger and her two cubs. The mother was sleeping with her head resting on the grass. One of the cubs was nestled close to her, while the other cub sat on her neck nibbling at her ear.

That's our picture.

Ian knew me better than anyone on the planet did. He knew my passion for cats, and my taste in furniture. Espresso finished night stands were on each side of the bed. On each of them stood identical lamps—coffee finished with faux leather shades. I looked at Ian and he could see how wide-eyed I was.

That's our furniture.

"I thought this would be a nice change." Ian seemed so happy for me. "And look, you have your own bathroom." Ian pointed to the door beside me, just after the entrance.

Frank pulled a 'Vanna White'. He opened the door, turned on the light, and introduced me to the bathroom with an outstretched arm and an animated hand.

Good grief!

"…a flat screen TV." Ian pointed at it. It was fixed on the wall directly in front of the bed.

That's our Plasma TV.

The Science Channel was on, and I knew Ian was doing his best to make me feel at home. He obviously had all of this shipped here, from Florida.

"This is the closet." Ian pointed at the last door in the room, next to a huge picture, slide-out window.

"Okay, I'll leave you guys alone and I'll see you tomorrow, Superman." Frank was still toying with me. He was standing behind me, but I did not turn around.

"Okay, Wonder Woman." I replied.

Frank walked out of the room and closed the door firmly as he exited.

"What was that all about?" Ian laughed.

"Do you really want to know?" I giggled back.

"Okay…yes," Ian protested. He had no clue, but I was about to show him.

Ian's eyes almost popped out of his head. He quickly walked toward me, but I put one hand up to stop him, while I propped myself up out of the wheelchair with the other. The bed was only a few feet away, and I reached it without a problem.

"James, that's great!" Ian was still concerned but at the same time, he was full of wonderment.

I propped myself up in the bed and leaned back on the headboard.

Tick…Tick…Jerk

Ian didn't know what to say. He stood there looking at me, and I could see he was bewildered.

"I will no longer be treated like an invalid." I said under a few long breaths. "I won't be in that wheelchair much longer."

Ian came and sat down close to me. I knew this was something he wished would happen especially after seeing me in a coma. For Ian, it was the longest year of his life, but now, I witnessed inspiring hope in his eyes.

"It's been two weeks of PT and I felt it was time to get the hell out of that chair." I insisted.

"I understand…I do…But…" Ian stumbled over his words.

I knew it was coming—The transformation back to guardian and protector. "Tonya was there with you, right?" Ian questioned.

"She was there until she had to go on a pee-break. Once she left, I looked at the parallel bars and that's all it took." Ian noticed how nonchalant I was about it. "She was gone for a few minutes and when she got back, she freaked out on me. After she got over herself, I made two passes between the parallel bars, and I plan on doing it again tomorrow!"

"Just promise me that you won't push yourself too quickly." Ian stressed.

I did not answer him. Instead, I took another moment to scan the room. Our tall espresso bureau stood beside the TV and on it was my portable CD/stereo. I noticed a bunch of CD's on a long shelf just above the bureau.

"All of that is ours." I pointed around the room. "You had all of this shipped from Florida?"

"Are you unhappy that I did this?" Ian's voice was a bit shaky.

"No Ian, this is great. I just have so many questions. Can you please be straight with me?"

***

From the beginning of our relationship, we became best friends. As time went by, our bond strengthened and we swore to always tell each other the truth. We were able to speak our minds and be entirely honest, no matter what. That was the golden rule and the bond that held us together for all these years. Although I had many questions for Ian, I wanted to tell him about my experiences—the ocean—the seal—Jade. **He'll think you are going insane!**

"We promised never to keep secrets." I pleaded.

Ian took a deep breath and let it out. He was very uneasy, and knew how I was about getting to the truth!

"What do you want to know?" Ian sat closer.

"I want to know everything." I replied.

The one person who never failed me, began to give me the missing pieces to this puzzle.

I will tell him about Jade, soon.

February 13, 2009
Friday 11:46 PM

Today's session did not go so well. The only thing missing from this unlucky day was a hockey mask and a hatchet. If I had access to the hatchet, I would have probably massacred the Doctor right there in her office! What a Friday the 13th! I met with Doctor O'Shea at 10AM for our session. Although Frank escorted me, I was taking each step on my own. I used the walker as my back up. This time Doctor O'Shea was already at her desk as we entered. She was on her phone and began to wrap up her call. She waved me in and said goodbye to whomever was on the phone. She had heard of my progress through Tonya, but now she could see for herself. I was standing on my own two feet.

"James, I am so happy to see you up and walking." She said, while hanging up the phone.

I left the walker beside her desk and sat down. "Almost there." I replied.

"Thank you Frank. I'll ring the nurse's station once we are done."

Doctor O'Shea seemed preoccupied and a bit tense. I sat in the chair and waited for her to start the session. She opened the top draw of her desk and out came a small recorder.

"James, I will be taping our sessions from now on." Doctor O'Shea informed me, then began recording.

Tick...Jerk...
She's looking!
"Are you comfortable with that?" She asked.
Do I have a choice?
I nodded and pretended I was okay with it. Doctor O'Shea began by recapping last week's session. She held the recorder close to her mouth and began reviewing the notes from her white pad. She went over my physical therapy treatment and went into detail on my progress. She cited the specific medication regimen and read aloud the notes taken by the head nurse.

"James has reported experiences of drowsiness, dizziness, loss of appetite, and feelings of isolation. Nurse's report states that James has shown periods of agitation, mood swings, moments of anxiety, and several instances of noncompliance."
Am I not sitting in front of you?
Doctor O'Shea went on and on, speaking into the recorder. I sat there and waited for her to finish. I decided to look out the window and it was snowing once again. I shook my head in disgust. Just looking at IT chilled me to the bone, and brought a cloak of depression down upon me.

"James?" Doctor O'Shea broke my daydream. "Are you okay?"

I turned away from the window and found her eyes. "Yes. I'm perfect."
Tick...Tick...
"So, tell me about your week." She inquired.

"As you can see, I have been working very hard with Tonya." I pointed at the walker. "I am feeling stronger every day."

"Yes, I see that. And I heard that you like your new room."

"Ian truly surprised me and I feel more comfortable." I began. "Did Ian tell you that we had a very long talk?"

I wanted to see where this would go. I knew Ian spoke with her. Frank gave me a heads-up. Ian had been in her office late yesterday evening, after I fell asleep. Frank implied that the meeting was a bit long. Frank went on to say that both he and Nurse Williams heard Ian and Doctor O'Shea raise their voices more than a few times. Ian was cursing and Frank said he wished he were a fly on the wall. This private meeting between Ian and the doctor lasted almost an hour.

"Yes, Ian informed me." The Doctor moved her chair closer to her desk, and placed the recorder down in front of me. "Can we revisit that conversation?"

Do I have to?

Doctor O'Shea gave me a moment, and then took it upon herself to force the issue. "For the record, I want to be clear. I have spent a great deal of time with Ian over the past year. I learned quite a bit about you, through Ian. Now that you are no longer in a coma, I wish to learn about you—from you."

I will cross my arms and she'll stop looking…

Tick…Jerk

I gave in. There was no way around it. I told her that Ian understood how I was feeling. Ian wanted me to feel more complete and relaxed. He gave the reasons why Boston was our only option, and apologized that I woke up in another state, during a snowstorm. Ian and I joked about that for a while, and I told him that I would get over it. It was easy to comprehend—CNS was the closest facility and the best match for me. Ian was able to transfer from his job in Florida to another branch here, and was able to rent a small apartment twenty-five minutes away from the hospital. He explained that the family was taking care of our house in Florida. I was happy to know, although we were no longer in Florida, that he and our cats were close by. He asked me to be patient. I promised to continue with the PT and continue to take my meds so he could eventually take me home. I told Doctor O'Shea that Ian and I discussed the accident, but had no luck with the missing pieces. I went on to tell her that I had apologized to Ian for all the pain I had caused him in the past. Although the diagnosis brought things into perspective, I still felt awful for my outbursts, crazy behavior, and volatile temperament. Ian was unwavering in his opinion and did not agree with me. He said I needed to stop beating myself up and insisted that I leave the past in the past and work on the future.

"It sounds like the two of you had a real heart-to-heart." Doctor O'Shea assessed.

"We did." I began. "It was easy for us to catch up a year's worth, in one hour. That's how well we know each other."

I held back and told her only what I wanted her to know. She was going to have to deal with it.

Control the ticking…Control the jerking…

"Yes, you and Ian share a special bond." Doctor O'Shea relaxed back in her chair. "Do you feel more grounded and less confused having heard the details of the past year?"

What kind of question was that? Was she listening to anything I said?

"I may not like the current situation, but at least I know why I am here. I will get stronger and soon I won't have to use that either." I pointed to the walker. "Soon Ian and I can get back to our lives in Florida."

"James, you understand that I cannot provide you with a timeline." She pronounced.

Terminal…I'm sorry Mr. Valvano…terminal…terminal…

Doctor Spinzer's voice rang in my head. I began to feel fidgety.

…Tick…Jerk…Jerk…

"James, did you hear me?" Doctor O'Shea was pushy.

"Yes, I know the disease is incurable and sooner or later I will die from it. I did the research." At that point, I was done, and wanted to go back to my room.

Doctor O'Shea noticed I was becoming annoyed. She was subtle, but once again, patronizing. "Ian did mention that you were proactive in helping your family understand many facets of the disease once your brother John was diagnosed."

What is your point?

"The bottom line James—we can only treat the symptoms. The medications only mask the disease."

Mr. Valvano…I am sorry…Terminal

"The medications can suppress the physical abnormalities."

Terminal…Mr. Valvano…I am so sorry…

58

"The medications can help suppress the anxiety...the depression..."

Sorry Mr. Valvano...Terminal...The test results...

I am here with you James...Breathe...Be strong...

"The medications will help you cope with the psychological and emotional..."

...I am here with you...

Test results...Test results...

"Your treatment is my main concern. Your mental health is paramount."

RED—WHITE—YELLOW—BLUE...BALLOONS

I FELT NOTHING...THE GROUND...THE SKY...DARTING GLASS...

Jerk....Jerk

"I want to help you understand what is happening to you..."

I could feel the sweat pouring down my face. The room was getting hotter and I felt the hammering of my heart.

Tick...Jerk...

Please stop! I am going to punch something! You Bitch!

"James, Ian wants to help, but I hope that he didn't cause a set-back."

Terminal...I am sorry Mr. Valvano...

"All of us here want what is best for you. Did Ian say anything else to you?"

Tick...Jerk...

My entire body was wet with perspiration. Doctor O'Shea's voice rang through the office, while the voices of Doctor Spinzer, and Jade echoed inside my head. One moment I was in the room with Doctor O'Shea, and the next I was strapped inside my tumbling vehicle.

"I've asked Ian to join our sessions if he'd like, but not to discuss anything without me present." Her voice continued to fill the office. "What else did Ian say?"

"Stop!" I screamed. "Stop!"

The room fell silent. She stood up from her desk, picked up the phone, and paged the nurse's station. She mumbled something into the phone, but I was too disoriented to hear her. I closed my eyes and wiped the perspiration from my face. I was humiliated as my saturated body sat in the chair. Doctor O'Shea didn't say a word, but walked around her desk and began to approach me.

"It will be fine. You'll be okay." She put her hand on my shoulder. "Just relax."

Jerk...Tick...

"Don't ever tell me what Ian can or cannot do." My tone was low and deep, and she clearly heard me.

She took her hand from my shoulder. I needed her to know that there was a fine line, which she could never cross. Ian was off limits and anyone who attempted to negate him in any way, would quickly be put in check.

"I didn't mean to upset you." Doctor O'Shea whispered, still standing behind me.

"Not a problem." I spoke sternly. "It would be best never to question Ian's intentions ever again." I paused. "We are clear, aren't we?" I added.

Frank and Nurse Clara came to the door. Frank instinctively came to my side, while Nurse Clara stood at the threshold with a wheelchair ready and waiting. I did not put up a fight. I had nothing left in me at that point, and walking back to my room was impossible. Doctor O'Shea walked back around her desk and sat down. I heard a 'click' sound; she stopped the tape recorder.

"Let me take you back to your room." Frank suggested.

This time I agreed with Frank and wanted him to hurry me out of there. I wanted to escape back to my room. Once there, I could pretend to be home, far from here. Frank and Nurse Clara placed my flaccid and sweaty body into the wheelchair.

Doctor O'Shea said nothing in the process. She continued to sit silently at her desk. Frank quickly took hold of the chair and we headed to the elevator.

"Frank, can you do me a favor?" I needed him to do as I asked.

"What do you need?" Frank asked without any reservations.

"Today I want to be alone. I want to stay in my room for the rest of the day." I ordered.

"What should I tell Ian?" Frank was concerned.

I whispered. "Tell him I need to think. He'll know exactly what I mean."

Tomorrow was not just Valentine's Day, but also our anniversary. Tonight I needed time to sort things out and get my head together.

***

After the out-of-control session with Doctor O'Shea, Frank brought me back to my room. He said that he would call Ian, and then he left. I wheeled myself to the bathroom and began to undress. I reached into the shower stall and turned on the water. My body had very little life left in it, however, I was able to stand up and transfer myself to the shower chair. The lukewarm water felt soothing as I began to wash away my thoughts and fears. I was able to reach deep inside to confront the pain, the anger, and the fear. I soaped and scrubbed my entire body, irrationally believing that I could remove the emotional pain and the physically uncontrollable ticking. I sobbed until it hurt, until I had no more tears. This disease was going to kill me. I thought I had accepted it, but now in my late thirties, I realized my chances of travelling and a life of independence was marginal. I had so many things I wanted to do. I had so many places I wanted to visit. I want to travel to the tropics, to Egypt, and so many other destinations. I want to experience so much more. I want out of this confined world. I want to give love and feel love without an expiration date. The only time I felt free was when I experienced the dreams…the visions. I want to close my eyes and return to the ocean where everything is safe, calm, and secure. I sat by the window for the remainder of the day. The only thing absent was Ian, a nice bottle of merlot, and a pack of Newport cigarettes.

I want a cigarette! No, I need a cigarette!

The medications were making me feel stoned. I missed sitting in the garage at home in Florida, smoking our Newport cigarettes. Ian would sit with me while I talked his ears off. I would strike up topic after topic, from life on other planets, to governmental conspiracies. Ian usually sat and listened to my warped concepts, yet sometimes he would give an opinion. The topic of discussion did not matter to him. Ian would give me his undivided attention. He would never judge me; he would just gaze into my eyes and hear me.

Yes, right now I would give anything for a Newport cigarette!
Tick...Tick...Jerk...Tick

Tonight I remained by myself. I was in my own private world, far from everyone. I played song after song on my stereo. I tried to make sense of the dreams—the visions...the ocean...the seal...my seal...Jade. Her voice would bathe away all of my pain, anger, and anxiety. Her voice was so warm and the best anesthetic. What was she telling me? Why am I feeling such a connection? Her presence numbed me from the inside out, and all negative emotions vanished. After sitting by the window for a while, I decided to stretch out on my bed. Ian stayed away tonight at my request. Tomorrow, I will fill him in on today's session with Doctor O'Shea. I cannot put my finger on it, but I feel something wrong, very wrong. I only hope that Ian notices it also. Nevertheless, tonight, I will fall asleep hoping to drift into the ocean, wishing Ian had not listened to Frank. Maybe Ian would come through that door. Maybe?

Where are you Jade? Please tell me what will happen.

February 14, 2009
Sunday 11:47PM

This morning I waited for Ian. After the nurse brought breakfast and the first round of medications, I started to worry and panic. It was 2PM on a Sunday, and Ian had not yet arrived.

Why would he show up? Maybe he finally had enough! Why be with me—the sick one!

It was just after lunch and Frank finally popped in to check on me. At first, I didn't say a word to him. I was so livid, and I was coming out of my skin.

"James? Are you okay?" Frank asked.

I was slowly pacing the room without the assistance of the walker. I heard Frank, but I felt like a volcano about to erupt.

Jerk...Tick...Tick

"Hello...James...What's up?" Once again, Frank tried to get my attention.

"I guess I'm not important enough. He's not here, I can't call him, and I am a burden. I shouldn't have told you to tell Ian to stay away. For Christ sake today is our anniversary! He's not coming to see me today. He's never coming back!" I yelled.

Frank came in and shut the door. He sat down in the guest chair and watched me pace. He continued to witness my anxiety, and listened to me yell and shout.

"So, are you going to tell me what this entire outburst of self-pity is about?" Frank asked.

I made it to the window and turned around. My heart was pounding and all I wanted to do was throw something—anything. I walked toward him.

Tick...Tick

"Frank, I'm not in the mood for your bullshit! If you want to play Psychiatrist, find someone else! Remember, that's the job of the woman upstairs. If you're going to be a pain in my ass, please do me a favor and get the hell out!" I snapped.

Frank sat back in the chair and crossed his arms. He looked at me for several seconds while I stood three feet in front of him.

"Doctor O'Shea probably asked Ian to stay away for a few days! Either that, or Ian finally came to his senses and realized he'd be better off without me!" I continued to flair.

Jerk...Tick...

"Had you given me a chance you would have understood why I came to see you." He reached into his pocket and handed me a folded piece of paper. I opened it and began to read the note.

Frank—
Please tell James that Ian called. He had to work today. Two of his employees called out and he is short staffed. Let James know that Ian will be here at the Center ASAP. Ian will also be bringing dinner.

Frank looked up at me. "If you had given me a minute all this could've been avoided."

Tick...Tick

I sat down at the foot of the bed and looked at Frank. I was ashamed, embarrassed, and felt like a total fool.

"I'm sorry for jumping all over you. I feel so edgy and I have a hard time controlling myself sometimes. I thought the meds were supposed to help." I let out a deep breath.

"Not a problem. I know you feel cooped up in here. You have to give the medication some time to work." Frank was kind. "It isn't unusual for the doctors to tweak one or two of the meds before they find the right levels. Try not to be so hard on yourself. I have an idea." Frank scratched his chin. "Why don't you go to the Recreation Room and find something to occupy your time before Ian comes?" Frank tried his best to make me feel less alone.

"Actually, do you have some free time? I would like for you to take me on a tour of this facility." I was plotting, and Frank didn't know why I wanted this favor. It was perfect timing.

"Yes, I have about thirty-five minutes. You want a tour?" Frank was a bit perplexed.

"Yes, a tour. Since I came out of the coma I haven't seen much of the facility." I began to weave my web.

Frank continued to listen to me, and I did everything I could to play it safe.

"I never heard of a Recreation Room? No one told me about that." I seeded.

Tick…Tick…Tick

"The Recreation Room is just behind the gym. There's a pool table, darts, air hockey, and a bunch of board games. They designed that room for patients and their families to visit. There's nice furniture in the sitting area and a flat-screen." Frank gave me a mental picture.

"Well it's not like I'll be using that space for any family visits. Frank, I am so lonely and in Doctor O'Shea's professional opinion, she won't let me call or see anyone in my family." I tried the sympathy card.

"I can understand how you must feel. Let's go to the Rec Room then."

"I am a bit tired. Can you take me in the wheelchair?" I exhaled hard and put my head down.

"Of course, let's go." Frank agreed.

I sat myself down in the chair and allowed Frank to take control of the wheelchair. We exited my room and began our journey to the first floor.

Pay attention and observe!

"Frank, I'm in room 201, right?" I asked him.

"Yes sir, the last room on this floor."

"How many rooms are up here and are they all like mine?" I treaded lightly.

"There are seven rooms here on the second floor. All the rooms have the same layout, but they allow the family or patient to redecorate." He was very informative.

I scanned every door as we passed by each, one at a time. Frank was slowly moving us toward the elevator. I noticed all seven rooms were occupied. The patient's names were listed in the same fashion as mine. I was one of seven.

"Doctor O'Shea probably believes treatment will be more affective for her patients if familiar surroundings are in place." Frank's opinion made perfect sense.

"It's so quiet in the other rooms." I dug a bit more.

"Well, there's reason for that." Frank responded.

"Well, are you going to tell me?" I asked.

Tick…Tick…Jerk

"I am not going to give you information about any patient here." He began. "Do you want me to lose my job?"

I'll find out on my own.

As we moved closer to the nurse's station, I noticed a white, double door straight ahead. I hadn't noticed it before. Above the double doors, there was a sign.

Unit—B

Each door had a window in each. Both doors wielded two red signs.

No Entry without I.D.
Electronic Entry Only—Swipe I.D.

Guests Must Sign In
Wait For Electronic Lock to Open

***

"How many units are in this part of the hospital?" I inquired.

We made it to the elevator and noticed a single nurse at the station. She was filing paperwork and talking on the phone at the same time. Frank pressed the down arrow and in seconds, the door opened. He wheeled me in backwards and pressed "1" on the panel. The door closed and he answered my question.

"There are four Units—A, B, C, and D. You are in Unit A." Frank outlined.

"So there are only seven of us in this one unit?" I questioned.

"Of course not," Frank corrected. "They're eight rooms on the first floor, which makes a total of fifteen beds in this Unit.

The elevator came to a stop and the door opened. Frank wheeled me out.

"If you turn here and walk down that hallway, there are four rooms." Frank pointed to the right side of the elevator. "There's a nurse's station directly around the corner."

"When Ian or other guests come to the facility, how do they get in?" I wanted more information.

"Right there," He pointed at the metal door right in front of us, "This door is the front entrance into this wing. All visitors sign-in with Ms. Tallen out there in the lobby."

I was making mental notes. It was apparent that opening the door without clearance was definitely problematic. Frank began to push the chair. The remaining four rooms were to the left of the elevator. I had a hard time remembering the layout. However, as soon as I saw the gym and the cafeteria, I remembered the row of rooms down the corridor.

"So where's the entry to the courtyard. I assume patients are allowed some fresh air." I continued to question him.

Jerk…Tick…Jerk

"The courtyard is directly down that hallway. It's just passed the last room. There's a small sitting area over there, and a staff member must escort the patient out to the yard."

Although I hadn't seen the door, I assumed some type of a keycard was necessary in order to open it.

"That's a bit drastic, don't you think?" I turned around in the chair and looked up at him. I took notice of his I.D. and a card of some sort attached by a metal clip on his shirt pocket. "It sounds more like a prison than a hospital, doesn't it?"

"I don't make the rules, I just abide by them." Frank responded. "Do you want me to take you into the Recreation Room?"

I waited a minute before giving him an answer. I peered into the gym and saw the Rec Room entrance next to Tonya's office.

"Actually Frank, I'm tired. Maybe I shouldn't push myself. Would you mind if we went back to my room?" I planned to come down later on, by myself, now that I saw what I needed to see.

"Not a problem. My shift is almost over for today. " Frank turned the chair around and we headed back to the elevator.

"I appreciate talking to you, and the mini-tour." Although I had a hidden agenda, I truly did not want to hurt Frank or cause him any trouble. He was actually a nice guy, and treated me as his equal, rather than just another sick-person. I knew he truly loved his job. He reminded me a lot of myself.

The elevator opened, and again Frank wheeled me in backwards. He hit "2" on the panel. I had to strike up a conversation. I wanted to change the topic quickly, so I asked him how long he'd been a nurse. He said he had been a nurse for almost six years and spent four of those years here at the CNS. He said he enjoyed his work and couldn't imagine doing anything else.

The elevator came to a quick stop on the second floor. He wheeled me back to my room and opened my door.

Jerk…Tick

"Okay then, I will see you tomorrow James." Frank began to turn and walk away, but stopped and looked back at me. "Before I go, I want to leave you with this. Whatever you are planning, think about it first. Don't do anything crazy."

Frank walked away. I wheeled myself inside and pushed the door closed behind me.

The only thing I am planning is getting out of here!

4:45PM

I honestly did not intend on meeting anyone this evening. I already gathered enough information from Frank earlier, but I actually did want to see the Rec Room. I knew I could get there with the help of the walker, but I decided to use the wheelchair just in case. I felt each of the medications slither their way into my system. I made my way to the elevator and pressed the down arrow. Of course, it took less than five seconds before Nurse Williams made her way around the station to strike up an unwanted conversation. She asked me how I was doing and wanted to know where I was headed. I wanted to tell her that I was about to set fire to this place and burn it down to the ground. Somehow, I knew that was not going to go over well. Therefore, I told her to mind her own business, and leave me the hell alone. The elevator door opened and I rolled myself in backwards. The door began to close and I was happily by myself. Soon, the door opened on the first floor, and I made my way down the short passageway and waited for the automatic doors to open. I entered the gym but no one was utilizing any of the machines. It was like a ghost town. I looked toward the far end of the room and could see Tonya through the huge pane of Plexiglas. She was sitting at her computer in her office. I wondered if I could make it by her door unnoticed, but that did not happen. By the time I made it to the Rec Room, she had already opened her door and stood there waiting for me.

"Hello James!" As anticipated, she was so overly excited. "What's up?"

I pointed to the Recreation Room door. "I just thought I'd check it out. Frank said I should try to keep myself busy."

"Absolutely," she exclaimed, "Roll closer to the door and it will open automatically."

I did as she advised and thanked her for her help. I wanted to tell her that I was still competent and able to read door signs, but instead, I smiled, bit my lip, and made my way into the room. I actually liked Tonya. She was another good egg, just like Frank. Being rude to her would have been unacceptable.

Before I could make it three feet inside, I noticed five Senior Citizens sitting at a round table. Up on the wall behind them was a large flat-screen TV. The volume was very low but I could see Wolf Blitzer interviewing someone via satellite. Across from the table stood a long shelving unit with every board game ever created. I moved closer to the shelving unit and noticed another round table further back in the room, just next to a deep burgundy, three-piece, sectional sofa. It didn't surprise me that the room had no windows. I made my way deeper inside, and found a pool table and four stools back toward the right corner of the room. I wheeled myself further along, and noticed there was another automatic door.

No Entrance
Without Physical Therapy Personnel

A smaller sign hung just below:

Hydrotherapy
Lap Pool Therapy

I was impressed and made a mental note to ask Tonya if I could utilize the facilities. I loved the water and a nice relaxing session in the hot tub was calling my name.

"Honey, aren't you going to introduce yourself?" A woman's voice rose from the front of the room.

I was hesitant to reply. I didn't feel up to sitting around with a group of geriatrics.

"Come on over honey, what's your name?" The woman spoke again.

I knew I had to suck it up, so I made my way toward their table. There were two men, and three women.

"Hi," I said, "My name is James."

The woman who called out to me spoke first.

"My name is Liz. This is Cathy, Kitty, Walter, and Mickey." She pointed at each of them as she called out their names.

"It's nice to meet all of you." I respectfully acknowledged them.

Mickey and Walter were playing checkers and didn't move their heads to say a word. I noticed Walter was in a wheelchair. A small oxygen tank stuck out from a backpack behind his chair, and tubes traveled from the tank to his nose.

"Jesus, aren't you going to say hello to James?" Cathy bellowed, and nudged Walter on his shoulder.

"For Christ's sake Cathy, can't you see I'm trying to beat this cheater?" Walter's voice was gruff. He took in a few heavy breaths from the oxygen tank.

"Cheater?" Mickey responded. "I am no cheater!"

"You are! I'm not going to take my eyes off of you!" Walter became more agitated.

"Don't mind them honey, they do this all the time." The woman named Kitty apologized for their behavior.

All three women agreed that each of the men were acting foolishly. They continued to chatter among themselves, complaining about Walter and Mickey's antics.

"The three of you can go to hell! You know this son-of-a-bitch cheats!" Walter interjected.

The room fell silent for a moment. The women yielded to Walter's foul mouth.

"Walter, how many times do we have to ask you to watch your language?" Cathy barked.

Walter grumbled something under his breath and gave the women a dirty look. Mickey stood up with the assistance of his cane, and began to walk out of the room.

"I am no cheater!" Mickey retorted. "It's not my fault if a third grader could beat your ass at a game of checkers!" Seconds later the automatic door closed behind him.

"James, they usually get along, but when they play games like this, they are so competitive." Liz added.

"If you ask me, they're just a couple of sex deprived, grumpy, old men." Cathy stated.

Liz and Kitty cackled loudly at Cathy's comment. I loved watching the entire scene.

"I can't believe that bastard left without finishing the game!" Yet again, Walter had to make waves. His breathing pattern was fast and heavy, and the intake of oxygen from the tank made an unsettling sound.

All three women gave him a look, and a disappointed headshake. Moments later, Walter released the brakes on his wheelchair and began to wheel himself to the door.

"Now don't make a stink about a silly little game." Cathy yelled just before the automatic door opened.

Walter didn't respond verbally, instead, he flipped them the bird, then wheeled himself through the door.

"Jesus, Mary, and Joseph," Liz began, "Someday Mickey is going to lose his socks and whack Walter over the head with his own oxygen tank!"

The girls began to laugh aloud. I had to control myself but it was next to impossible.

"Either that, or Walter will bludgeon Mickey to death with his cane!" Cathy rebounded.

The laughter was intoxicating, and I pictured myself on the set of a hilarious *Golden Girls* episode. These three women were completely off their chains.

"I don't know about you girls, but it's time for me to watch my soaps." Kitty mentioned, still laughing. "I have to catch up."

The three women got up from the table and began to leave the room. Cathy informed me that she was in room 203, Kitty was in room 204, and Liz was in room 205. She paused for a moment, and then stated that Mickey was in room 206, and Walter occupied 207.

"You can come by anytime," Cathy began, "just knock on our doors and if we are in we'd love for you to visit."

"Most of the time I am knitting or sowing." Kitty said.

"If that's what you call it." Liz joked. "I usually read most of the time."

"Just don't allow Cathy to bore you to death." Kitty started. "She has hundreds of picture albums of her children, grandchildren, and great-grandchildren. She'll tell you story after story and you'll wish you were dead." Kitty laughed.

They continued to banter with one another and waved before exiting the room. I sat there for several minutes after they left. The room was quite, but I relished the fact that I was no longer alone inside this prison. I was going to take them up on their offer and visit each of them.

"James, so what do you think of the Recreation Room?" Tonya came in but I was in a daze, still amused by the geriatric squad.

"I'm sorry Tonya?" I looked up at her.

"The Rec Room…isn't it something?" She asked again.

"Oh, yes…it is very nice. I noticed you have a hydrotherapy tub and a small pool back there." I pointed over my shoulder. "I'd love to use both of them."

"Not a problem. I think you'll be up to it soon." Tonya declared, "Also, I just thought you'd want to know that Ian is up in your room."

I did not hesitate. I gave her a smile and wheeled myself out of the room.

"Enjoy your evening!" Tonya yelled.

I knew I had to do one thing before heading back to my room to see Ian. I made my way toward the elevator, and continued to the lobby access door. I carefully stood up from the wheelchair and looked through the thick window on the door. I noticed two security guards in the lobby, and an older woman sitting at a desk close to the facility entrance. I tapped on the glass, hoping to get the attention of one of the guards. I tapped with my knuckle once again, and one of the guards came to the door.

Pay attention!

I backed away from the door and pushed the wheelchair behind me. The door opened and the guard stuck half of his body inward. I looked quickly at his badge.

"Is everything okay?" He asked. On his badge was—Mr. Steel.

"I'm sorry to bother you Mr. Steel, but I was wondering if you saw Frank?" I asked.

"Frank left earlier this afternoon. Do you need me to call a nurse?" Mr. Steel was authentically concerned.

"No, that's fine. I'll just head up to my room. I forgot that Frank told me he was leaving earlier today. Thank you." I stepped back and sat down into the wheelchair.

Mr. Steel stood there for a few seconds then entered back into the lobby. The door closed and I hurriedly made my way toward the elevator.

I will have to plan this cleverly!

This is not the way James. The way out is not through that door.

Now on the second floor, I wheeled myself as fast as I could down the hallway toward my room. I wanted to apologize to Ian for last night. My door was closed, and I slowly turned the handle and wheeled myself in. Ian was sitting at a small round table waiting for me.

Celine Dion was singing on the CD player while a white candle sat in the center of the table. The ambiance was perfect and everything looked great. I wheeled myself to the small table. A group of Valentine balloons floated beside the bed and an envelope with my name on it was attached to one of the ribbons. Ian knew how much I loved Celine Dion. I didn't care if people thought of it as 'a gay thing'. They needed to live it, learn it, love it, and then get the hell over it!

Ian spoke softly. "Happy Valentine's day, and happy anniversary."

Ian had cooked. It was his favorite thing to do. I looked at the plates and he had prepared shrimp scampi, butterfly shrimp, a nice cut of filet mignon wrapped in bacon, and rice pilaf.

"Yes Ian, Happy Valentine's day, and happy anniversary." I replied.

"You look very nice." Ian noted.

I was wearing jogging pants and my orange, Reese's Peanut Butter t-shirt. It obviously didn't matter to him. He was just happy to see me, and accepted me completely.

"I actually shaved myself today. It took forty-five minutes, but I used my left hand to hold and guide my right hand. I didn't slit my throat, so that's a plus!"

Ian smiled. "So, are you tired of the nurses doing it?"

Ian understood my frustration. I hated shaving. For the past seven years, I have maintained a tight beard and goatee. However, each time the nurses tried to keep it as defined as I requested, they would inevitably botch the shave each time!

"Well, I wanted to give it a try. Frank shaved me the last few times and got it right." I mentioned.

"Well, it looks fine." Ian complemented. "Are you ready to eat?"

He did not have to ask me twice. Although the food here at the facility wasn't half-bad, nothing came close to Ian's cooking.

"I know you would have wanted a bottle of Merlot, but with the medications…" Ian tried to explain.

"Everything is fine," I cut in. "No worries. I am happy with bottled water. Maybe you can take me outside for a nice cigarette?"

Ian did not reply, but began to cut his steak. We began to eat our celebratory dinner. I closed my eyes for a split second, and it felt like we were home. Everything tasted phenomenally. We began to share some small talk about his job and my physical therapy. The conversation was light and pleasant. This was not the right time to say or do anything to ruin this evening, especially if the conversation had anything to do with Doctor O'Shea.

"Oh, I wheeled myself downstairs to check out the Rec Room. To my surprise I met some of the funniest people." I informed him.

"Who?" Ian asked.

"Well, they are in their late sixties, early seventies, and funny as hell! There are three women—Cathy, Liz, and Kitty. The other two are men—Mickey, and Walter."

Ian continued to eat while I spoke. I told him that I thought the two men were going to have a throw-down. I explained that they were playing checkers and Walter accused Mickey of cheating. I mentioned how perturbed the women were when Walter cursed Mickey out.

"They were funny Ian. Each of them has a room here on the third floor. They asked me to visit them whenever I wanted."

"So, they are up here?" Ian was surprised.

"Yes, and I can't wait for you to meet them. They're a panic!"

"Hopefully I will." Ian replied.

"The only other person I haven't seen again was this one young woman." I gave Ian the details of the first day of PT. I saw her at one of the machines, and was happy to see someone close to my age. At that moment, it made sense that the last remaining room on this floor had to be hers.

"Well maybe you'll get to meet her too." Ian speculated.

Our conversation was shortly interrupted by a knock at the door. Nurse Williams came in with a cupful of medications.

"I'm sorry to intrude, but it's that time again." She pointed out.

She emptied the cup into my hands and waited for me to take each one.

There's nothing better than being treated like a five year old!

She left the room and Ian and I continued to enjoy our dinner. We spoke about our cats, and laughed. It wasn't long when I noticed Ian looked tired. Working a full-time job and coming here every day was taking its toll on him. We cleaned off the table and Ian placed everything in a cooler. I was feeling tired myself, but asked if he would stay with me for a little while longer. He waited for me to fall asleep.

***

10:54PM

I opened my eyes and Ian was gone. He had blown out the candle and switched on the nightstand light. Right beside me, he left the card. I opened it and read the wonderful words. He always knew how to pick out the best card for any occasion. I stared at his handwriting for quite some time. I became frightened. As I sat on the edge of the bed, I feared that moment. I feared he moment when a man named Ian would come to visit, and I would fail to recognize him.

February 20, 2009
Friday—11:21PM

This morning did not begin the way I had planned. It was still very dark when I woke. It had to be around 4:45AM. A sudden noise jolted me from a sound sleep. Someone slammed a door. The only light in the room was coming from the television. I always slept with it on. I second-guessed what I heard and tried to fall back to sleep. I turned onto my right side and looked up at the television. As usual, the Science Channel was on. It didn't matter how many times I saw repeat after repeat, if it had anything to do with Egypt, the planets, or ET's, I would watch it again. I rested my eyes and tried to fall back to sleep when it happened again.

Who is slamming their goddamned door?

I got out of the bed as quickly as I could and went to put on my robe. It happened yet again. SLAM! I struggled to get to the door, and felt adrenalin flow through my veins. I slowly opened the door just enough to peer out into the hallway. In the corridor light, I saw them.

That voice! Why do I remember that voice?

"You better stay away from me!" The girl demanded.

"Don't make me call Doctor O'Shea this early in the morning!" The night nurse blared, but I still couldn't see anyone clearly.

"Go to hell and stay out of my room!" The young woman screamed.

78

Confirmed! Mystery girl is in room 202! That's the younger woman in the gym!

I heard the nurse's footsteps, as she turned and hustled down the hallway. Before I could close my door, she saw me.

"Come over here, hurry!" She whispered sharply.

Adrenaline did not afford me a moment to think. Instinctively, I opened my door and walked toward hers.

Tick...Tick

"Get in here." The young woman pulled me by my left arm and dragged me into her room. "We don't have much time."

The bathroom light bathed her room. Frank was right. Each room on this floor shared the same layout. She closed her door and there we stood.

"There are three cameras on this floor." She began. "There's one at each end of the hallway, and another facing the elevator from behind the nurse station. There are cameras all over this place! They watch our every move! I have to get out of this place!"

"What is going on? Why are you freaking out, and what was happening with that nurse?" I tried to keep my voice down.

"That nurse is calling security on me again. They'll put me upstairs in one of those holding rooms next to Doctor Psycho's office." She was acting paranoid, which made me feel quite uncomfortable.

Jerk...Tick...Tick

"I'm leaving." I informed her, and went to open the door.

"They are killing us...We are not safe." She whispered.

I stopped with my hand on the doorknob, turned around and looked at her.

"You have to help all of us." She had a wicked and frantic look in her eyes.

Tick...Jerk...Tick

"What is your name?" I asked.

"Sarah." She quickly answered. "So, are you going to help us?"

"What's going on? Why are you acting like this?" She was making me feel edgy.

Her voice! It was her at the elevator...and that night in my

room!

"Wait a minute! It was you! You came to my room that night. Why did you say this place was Hell?"

I stood there for a short time, listening while Sarah spoke. She told me that she had been here at CNS for over two years. Her parents and two sisters hadn't visited her in almost a year. According to Sarah, her family abandoned her and moved away. Her opinion was cut and dry; this place was indeed Hell, and each of the Staff was Doctor O'Shea's (The Devil) disciples.

"They'll be here any second. Before you go, be very careful what you say and who you talk to. Trust no one, not even the almighty Doctor O'Shea." Sarah was truly spooking me.

"Are you going to be okay? What are they going to do to you?" At that moment, I became very worried. Although I just officially met Sarah, I feared her, but was very concerned for her safety. Nevertheless, I wanted to know more. I wanted to hear what she knew about this place.

"I'll be fine." She exclaimed. "Don't forget that each move we make is being videotaped." Sarah's paranoia suddenly made its way into my own psyche, and the thought of someone, somewhere looking at my every move, was sick!

"Okay, calm down." I placed my hand on her shoulder. "I'm going to go back to my room now. Please try to meet me in the cafeteria tomorrow around 11AM. We'll speak more about this then."

I opened the door and moved as fast as I could to my room. Before I could close the door behind me, I heard two men and the night nurse talking. They were getting closer to Sarah's room. I continued to peek out my door. One of the security guards knocked first, and then both of them entered Sarah's room. I closed my door, and placed my ear firmly against it. A moment later, I heard a struggle, and Sarah began cursing and screaming. I heard a "slap" sound. A few seconds later, I heard it two more times.

Oh my God! They are hitting her!
Jerk…Tick…Tick

My heart was pounding and my mouth went dry. One second I heard

Sarah, and then everything fell silent. I panicked, but could not do a thing to help her. I opened my door again and tried to see what was happening. I made sure they wouldn't notice that I was there, witnessing what they were doing to her. The nurse had a syringe in her hand, while the two security guards placed Sarah into a wheelchair. The nurse and both guards moved down the hallway, with Sarah in the chair. I stood there in horror. I could not believe what I was seeing.

Jesus, what is wrong with this place?

I closed the door and headed for the bed. I didn't remove my robe, and all I wanted was to hide myself under the covers.

Ian, I wish you were here!

I pulled the covers over my head and tried to calm down. Not being able to call Ian when I needed him the most, was hard for me to accept.

He'd sneak your cell phone in. Just ask him!

The first round of meds was coming soon. No matter what I tried to do—think positive thoughts, count sheep, nothing was going to help me get back to sleep. I pulled myself out from under the blanket and leaned back on the headboard.

Cameras in the hallway…they see everything?

Then it hit me. Today was my regularly scheduled appointment with Doctor O'Shea at 10 AM. Even after a full night of sleep, free from any traumatic episodes, I was never entirely ready to sit face to face with her. Considering the drama I just experienced, the best possible strategy for an uneventful session is to stay calm and tell her what she wants to hear. I heard Sarah's voice inside my head.

Don't trust anyone! Watch what you say! Don't trust Doctor O'Shea!

I sat up in bed until something came over me. I became incredibly tired, and within seconds, I was gone.

10 AM

Ten O'clock came sooner than I had hoped for, and once again, I sat waiting for Doctor O'Shea. Frank just left and assured me that the Doctor would be along in just a little bit.

How is this session going to go?

I tried to stop myself from yawing—constantly. After this morning's event with Sarah, I was utterly exhausted. My left arm was sore and it took me a few minutes to remember that Sarah pulled me into the darkness of her room. Nurse Clemins woke me this morning to administer my meds. I sat up in the bed and examined my arm. I saw what looked like a handprint. The nurse handed me the cup of medication, waited for me to empty the cup into my mouth, then gave me some water.

"Busy morning?" She placed her hand on her hip. "I can tell you didn't get much sleep. You have some serious luggage under those eyes." I saw her look at my arm. She noticed the bruise.

"Yes, I had a very busy morning, and no I didn't sleep well at all." She got under my skin. "I was too busy making angels outside in the snow! But, the highlight of my morning was when I stripped down to my birthday suit, and had a snowball fight with my friend Frosty!"

I looked at her and waited for her response. Instead, she rolled her eyes and left the room.

10:13 AM

"Gosh James, I had a few things to straighten out. I'm sorry I am late." Doctor O'Shea seemed flustered.

She moved behind her desk and followed the same routine. Once she finished putting on her white coat, she sat down. I watched as she opened her briefcase and removed the palm-sized tape recorder, white pad, and my folder. Once she got herself in order, she began recording our session.

"You look very tired this morning. I understand that there was an issue last night?" She had a different tone to her voice. Something was definitely off.

" I woke up to the sound of a door slamming, voices outside my door, so of course I wanted to make sure everything was okay." I did my best to play it safe.

Doctor O'Shea did not say a word. She just she sat a stared at me.

"So how is she, Sarah?" I asked.

Doctor O'Shea jotted down a few notes. "James, I will not discuss this with you."

Really? You can't even tell me if she's okay.

"Sarah seemed very afraid and basically wanted to be left alone." I tried again.

"I believe it is best to focus on you right now." Doctor O'Shea clearly wanted no part in discussing anything pertaining to Sarah.

Jerk...Tick...Tick

I pushed the subject. "It is obvious that you know I went to her room. I only stayed for a few minutes before returning to mine. That's when I saw the guards and the night nurse take her away in a wheelchair. Sarah told me that there are cameras in the hallway and one at the elevator." I wanted Doctor O'Shea to explain what happened.

"For security reasons there are three cameras on each of the floors. We have placed two in the gym, two in the Recreation Room, three in the cafeteria, and one in the Hydrotherapy room."

As the Doctor informed me on the Security Camera layout, she continued to take notes.

You have to get that folder! You have to get into that cabinet!

"Tonya has stated in her report that you are doing much better than she anticipated." She completely switched the topic.

"Yes, I am up and about most of the time without the walker. Today, Frank walked with me to your office. I really feel stronger." I tried to diffuse the tension in the room.

"Tonya also wrote in her report that you wheeled yourself to the Rec Room. How come you didn't walk?"

Tick...Jerk

"I was a bit drained and wanted to go alone, so I figured it would be best to take the chair." I answered.

I was wondering where she was going with these questions. Instead, I didn't give her time to speak. I explained to her that I met Tonya at her office and we spoke. I pointed out that Tonya was happy I decided to visit the Rec Room, and was pleased to see that I was venturing out. I then told the doctor that I had met the other residents—Cathy, Liz,

Kitty, Walter, and Mickey. The entire time I spoke to Doctor O'Shea, she continued to write.

"How long did you visit the Recreation Room?" She broke in.

"Not long at all. We introduced ourselves, however Mickey and Walter were arguing over a game of checkers. Walter accused Mickey of cheating, and the women had a fit because Walter used strong language. I thought it was absolutely funny."

"What happened then?" Doctor O'Shea pressed.

"Well, it wasn't long until both Walter and Mickey left. The ladies stayed behind for a little while, and extended an invite if I ever wanted to visit with them in their rooms. It's great because we are all on the same floor." I was excited.

"Tonya said that you asked her to use the hydrotherapy facilities." Doctor O'Shea seemed to have difficulty staying on topic. Why was she all over the board today?

"Yes, Tonya said I'd be able to use the hot tub, and the pool." Just thinking of the hot tub made me feel relaxed.

"Let's move on." Doctor O'Shea was acting weird. "This week's nurse's report specifies that you have been compliant when taking your medication. However, a few of the nurses stated that you will not allow them to shave you, nor monitor you while showering."

Jerk...Jerk...Tick

"I walked to your office this morning independently, didn't I?" I waited for her to reply.

"Yes. You did, James." Her voice was plain and simple.

"I did not require assistance from anyone. I asked Frank to walk with me, and he didn't hover over me like the rest of them. He waits for me to ask for his help. I am able to go to the bathroom by myself, so why do I need them to shave and monitor me in the shower?" I declared.

"So, you have completed your rehabilitation?" She went there again. I had never been this annoyed at one person. I wanted to throw her phone across the room.

"No, I never said that!" I beamed. "Why do you always treat me like a child?"

Doctor O'Shea didn't respond. She sat there looking at me—peering at me. I despised her 'holier-than-thou' attitude.

I tried again to explain. "Listen, I have nothing against the nurses. I can shower myself without any assistance, and if I need help shaving, I ask Frank. The other nurses can't get it right and they always screw it up. If I wanted a bloodbath, I'd shave myself!"

She continued to look at me, and then began to scan through the nurse's notes. "Yes, Frank noted that in his weekly report." She paused. "Although, another report states that you continue to show hostility toward certain nurses." She looked up at me. "Can you explain?"

Tick...Jerk...Jerk...

This session with Doctor O'Shea felt synonymous to a visit to the principal's office. I had no clue what this was about, and she was working on my last nerve.

"Before I answer that, what did Frank write in his report regarding my attitude? What did Frank write about me?" Frank and I have our own way of co-existing, and I wanted to hear his report, from her mouth.

"Frank didn't have any negative comments." She admitted.

"Then I suggest you hold a meeting with the other nurses. Explain to them that I do not appreciate being treated like an invalid. Let them know that it completely ticks me off when they try to invade my space, and my business. Frank treats me with respect and knows how to talk to me."

Doctor O'Shea raised her eyebrows and tapped her pen on the desk. I knew she was becoming upset with me. Her face became red, and I could see the veins in her neck restrict.

She spoke. "Is there anything else you would like me to do? I am here at your beck-and-call. You can make a list and I will personally cater to all of your requests." She laid the sarcasm on pretty thick, which sent me over the edge.

Jerk...Tick...Jerk

I was over her, and I had enough. I was tired and completely sick of her crap. She didn't know sarcasm, the way I did.

She continued. "Please let me know how we can better assist you.

Whatever you want…whatever you need, please let me know…Your wish is my command."

What a bitch!

Ask and you shall receive. I gave her my requests. "Actually, there are a few things you could do for me. I would like you to allow Ian to bring me my laptop, several books, and of course, once a week I want him to bring my cats for a visit. I'll give you some time to fulfill my wishes. If you need any clarification, feel free to visit my room, or send one of your nurses!"

I stood up and I left her sitting in her chair. I was done with her nasty remarks and ridiculous line of questions. I started to walk out.

"This isn't helping, James!" Doctor O'Shea yelled. "Our session isn't over!"

I turned back around and glared at her. "You are right. None of this is productive or helpful. Next week, try not to be such an irritating bitch! And yes, our session is over!"

I slammed the door behind me and made my way back to my room.

Don't trust anyone, especially her!

1:11 PM

I could not wait to speak with her. I hoped that Sarah remembered to meet me in the cafeteria. I made my way down the hall, knowing each step I took was videotaped. I waved nicely at the nurses and gave them a huge, fake smile. The elevator opened and I entered. Before the doors closed, I waved at the camera.

I need to tell Ian!

The elevator let me out to the first floor and I quickly passed the gym, and then entered the cafeteria. As I made my way to the lunch trays, I scanned the room. A handful of people were scattered throughout the room. I suddenly became disappointed.

Tick…Jerk…Jerk

I needed to see her. I needed to talk to her. I pushed my tray along the silver rails and placed a sandwich, a bag of pretzels, a bowl of strawberries, a fork, and a diet coke down onto the tray.

Tick…Jerk

I tried not to spill or drop anything, as I made my way to a table in the far corner of the cafeteria. My biggest goal today was to make it to the table without ticking and making a total ass out of myself. I succeeded, however I wanted nothing more than the ticking and jerking to stop. If I heard another person mention that I had to give the medications time to work, I would lose my mind! I made it over to an empty table, placed my tray down, and slipped into the chair. I began to eat my sandwich and thought about my visit with Doctor O'Shea this morning. I didn't want to be so combative and rude, but the entire session was worthless. I knew I stirred the pot again, but what does she want from me?

Ian won't be mad. He'll understand.

"Don't look at me. We can't let them see that we are talking." Sarah whispered.

She startled me and at the same time, I was glad to see her. Sarah sat four seats away from me on the opposite side of the table.

"I didn't think you were going to show up." I whispered back. I kept my eyes on my tray.

"Well I'm here. I just got done with the White-Witch-Psychiatrist." Sarah snarled.

I filled Sarah in on my visit this morning with Doctor O'Shea. Sarah listened to the entire event and especially enjoyed what I said to the doctor on the way out of her office. Sarah seemed restless. I personally understood why. A visit with Doctor O'Shea would have that effect on a cadaver.

"I told you that you shouldn't trust anyone, and that definitely includes her!" She protested.

Tick…Jerk

"I only speak with Frank, and he seems very trustworthy." I whispered back. I tried not to look at her.

"No one!" She darted. "Trust absolutely no one. They all report back to her!"

"Okay. I won't confide in anyone, but why?" I needed her to explain.

"I've been in here for a long time. I've seen and heard many things. We are in Unit A." Sarah paused for a moment and nonchalantly turned her head to scan the room. It was clear and she continued to speak. "I know you have the same disease as I do. The other units specialize in other diseases like Alzheimer's, Parkinson's, Lou Gehrig's, and the list goes on."

"Okay, I still don't get your point. How can you assume we have the same disease?" I was confused. I couldn't make the connection.

"Let me finish." She muttered. "I've seen at least eight patients leave this unit in body bags. I found ways to confirm their diseases."

Sarah was utterly freaking me out. I placed my sandwich down and continued to listen to her. Her voice was intense and quite conspiratorial.

She went on. "When you head back to your room, before entering the elevator, I want you to quickly take a look into the Reception area. It's the main entrance into the building. You'll soon find out that we on lock-down in this unit!"

"I actually spoke with one of the guards." I acknowledged.

Jerk...Jerk

"So, your friend hasn't told you yet?" Sarah was suggesting something and I was unsure if I wanted to know. I didn't answer her and wished Ian was here.

"Let me fill you in." Sarah's tone changed. "I found out the hard way. CNS is a different kind of facility."

"I know this. Ian already went over that with me." I tried to explain.

"I'll make this easier for you." Sarah pushed her lunch tray to the side. "We all have spacious rooms and can decorate it as we wish. We eat decent meals, unlike the atrocious crap served in typical hospitals. We get therapy, both physical and mental, and receive medications. Everything is free, with strings attached of course."

Subconsciously, I did not want to admit it to myself, but Sarah was venturing down a path I already entertained. Ian mentioned CNS was

88

the closest facility in the country, and pointed out that this establishment specializes in neurological diseases. It was a "research facility."

Tick…Tick

"Did Ian tell you their policy? Did he mention their rights?" This time Sarah looked me straight in the eyes. "Ask him when you see him tonight."

I heard what she was saying but I did not want to consider it.

"You saw what they did to me, didn't you?" She looked at me with her piercing eyes.

"I did…I mean yes, I heard…but I don't understand." I became tongue-tied and I felt knots build within the pit of my stomach.

Tick…Jerk

"I know you did! They are experimenting on us!" Sarah's voice rose. "From the moment you entered this place, your friend Ian and your family signed you over to them! CNS owns us!"

"I can't accept that. Ian would never allow it." I protested.

"And, you know Doctor O'Shea isn't what she claims to be." Sarah slid across three chairs, and was now sitting directly in front of me. "Your only hope is Ian, and you better make sure he's on your side. He is our last hope to get out of here. He has to report what they are doing!"

"You are right about the doctor. She's not my favorite person, but she's still a doctor!" I struggled with Sarah's theory. "I don't like her at all, but she couldn't be part of whatever you're suggesting."

"Just make sure you tell your friend everything!" Sarah grabbed my hand. "Everything!" She hissed. "If the disease doesn't kill you, they will!"

I could tell by her demeanor, that Sarah was very volatile and outright suspicious of anything that moved or breathed. Why wouldn't she be this unsettled? Her own flesh and blood abandoned her. Was she telling the truth? Was she jealous because she had no one, and I had Ian?

"Here he comes." Sarah whispered. "Don't forget to talk to Ian. We can't afford for you to screw this up!" She frantically picked up her tray and hustled away.

I turned and saw Frank walking toward me.

"So, it's great to see that you have stopped living the life of Riley. The nurses must be thrilled that you decided to get your own lunch today." Frank was so annoying, yet he knew how to make me smile.

"Please tell me you didn't find me just to set me off." I grinned.

"I can't believe that you are actually here in the cafeteria. You finally decided to join the rest of us." Frank seemed more upbeat than usual.

"Yes, I decided to join the second class citizens." I played.

As we were talking, I wondered if Sarah was watching. Was she listening? Was she monitoring me? Was she waiting for me to turn her in?

"So what are your plans for today?" Frank inquired, snapping me back into place.

"I am waiting for Ian to show up." I started. "Frank, can I ask you a question?"

"It never stopped you before, so shoot." Frank sat down in the chair next to me.

Tick...Jerk

"Hypothetically speaking, if you witnessed a patient being abused, what would you do?" I did not look at frank directly. I felt uncomfortable asking him.

"Why would you ask me a question like that?" Frank whispered, and I noticed how appalled he became.

I realized it was too late to take back my question, and if I tried, Frank would not let it go.

"I'm not following you James. What's going on?" Frank wanted more information.

"I'm not sure if you know about this, but Sarah was pulled out of her room last night by two guards, and a nurse shot her up with a sedative." I looked at Frank and he said nothing. He was waiting for me to continue.

"Frank, she did nothing wrong. I watched as they took her from her room."

Frank remained silent. He absorbed everything I said, but continued to stare at me.

"Hello." I tried to get him to respond. "Frank?"

Frank took a deep breath. "James, I truly think you should stay out of this one. Literally leave it alone, and do not mention it to anyone!" Frank was serious, and I was actually shocked by his response.

Tick…Jerk

Frank moved in closer. "James I promise you, there is no abuse going on here. You didn't see anything. Leave it alone. Trust me."

"Frank, I saw it with my own eyes, and as a matter of fact, Sarah told me this happens to her at often!" I raised my voice. "And it's true, isn't it? The doctors can do anything to us, can't they? That's the agreement, isn't it?"

It became clear to me, there was a strong possibility Frank was about to sweep this under the carpet.

He's like the rests of them!

"James, do you trust me?" Frank asked.

"You've given me no reason to mistrust you Frank, but now I'm a bit leery." I muttered.

"Let Doctor O'Shea handle this." Frank was serious. "Can you do that for me?

"Okay, but if it happens again, I'll come looking for you! I will blow the lid off of this!" I made myself clear.

Frank stood up from his chair and put one hand on my shoulder.

"Anytime you need to talk, I'll be here." Frank reassured me. "I am here anytime, James."

He turned and maneuvered his way toward the automatic doors. I looked at my lunch tray and ultimately lost my appetite. I had to get with Ian. Before I decided to leave the table, Sarah's words clouted my mind.

Did Ian tell you their policy? Did he mention their rights? Ask him when you see him tonight."

I only hope, and assume that Ian will be forthcoming. If not, I will do whatever it takes to find out the truth about this place.

Can you trust Ian?

February 21, 2009
Saturday 11:27PM

I needed something to do. I needed to experience something positive today, especially after the unproductive meeting with Doctor O'Shea. I decided to find Kitty, Cathy, and Liz. I felt it was time to get to know each of them. It was just after lunch. I left my room, and knocked on Liz's door. I waited a couple of minutes before knocking again. Before I got the chance, the door opened and Liz greeted me.

"Well good morning James." Liz was exceptionally perky. "It's nice to see you, come in." Her voice was a bit scratchy, but very welcoming. She hurried me inside then closed the door.

I walked inside and instantly noticed that Liz tried to mask the smell of a cigarette, with a sweet perfume. I wasn't quite sure if I was shocked, or eager to know that she had access to cigarettes. I walked further into the room and noticed the window was cracked, and a small Dixie cup rested beside it. Liz walked ahead of me, grabbed the cup, and hurriedly entered the bathroom. Seconds later I heard the toilet flush. She closed the bathroom door and looked at me.

"You won't say anything, will you?" Liz's voice cracked again.

"Honey your secret is safe with me." I replied. She saw the smile on my face and it set her at ease. I wanted so badly to ask her if she had an extra cigarette, but somehow it didn't feel right.

"I don't give a damn what they say!" Liz laughed and coughed at the same time. "Come, sit down."

Before making our way to the small table, I noticed the small piano nestled in the crook of the room. It sat in the opposite corner from the table. I was drawn to the fixture, and made my way over to it. Upon a beautiful rectangular cloth, pictures of all sizes rested within their frames. Their presence was overpowering. Although I didn't know who they were, faces of every age looked up at me. They looked into my eyes and tried to look into my soul.

"They are my family." Her voice whispered from over my shoulder. "Many memories fill those picture frames."

I didn't respond. I found myself overtaken and then I touched it. I placed my hand on the piano. Electric surged through my body—it was a soothing and warming rush. I touched the frames and again, I looked into the eyes of her family members. Strange it was—very strange, and I felt myself wanting more.

"Honey, come and sit with me." Liz spoke again, and I turned to see her warm face.

I made my way over to the table, and we sat. I was at ease with Liz right away, and I couldn't shake the uncanny feeling. She was a strong woman. I could tell she was a woman of intelligence, with conviction and such fortitude. The way she sat, and the way she spoke, made me believe that she was the type of person who remained focused and unhinged. She definitely had her share of life's hardships, but her eyes told another tale. They spoke of family, love, pride, and happiness. Her eyes were filled with stories, and I wanted to read every one of them.

"It is so good to see you," Liz began. She reached out and grabbed my hand. "I was thinking about walking down to the Recreation Room later today."

FLASH

The white light hit my eyes and made my body jerk backward. I felt her hand in mine; however, I was now sitting on her lap. I was a young boy, and we were travelling inside a vehicle. We were driving on a highway, and the cars were moving very fast on either side. She held my hands tightly and began to laugh. Her deep laugh, mixed with a tickling cough, was distinct. She was playing paddy-cake with the little boy—with me. Where we were going was unknown, but I sat comfortably on Liz's lap. I was so happy in her presence and I could see the love she had for me. It was there in her eyes and in her playful manner. She hugged the little boy—she hugged me, and I listened to her laugh as it filled my heart.

FLASH

"Honey, are you okay?" Liz asked. We were back in her hospital room.

"Yes, I'm sorry…what did you say?" I tried to snap out of the sudden and bewildering visualization.

"I was just wondering if you would meet us down in the Recreation Room sometime this afternoon." Liz responded, still holding my hand. "I know everyone would love to see you again."

"I may do that." I quickly replied. The vision was still nudging me. I was puzzled and couldn't process what just happened. Whatever I had just experienced, emotionally and physically drained me.

"Good, it would be nice." Liz stated, and then released my hand from her grasp. "Honey, I have an appointment with Doctor O'Shea so I have to get ready. I also have to air out this room before they come for me!" She laughed and coughed at the same time.

"I understand." I smiled and stood up. "I hope to see you soon."

"Anytime honey." Liz gave me a hug and once again, I felt like a little boy cradled in familiar arms.

Liz walked me to the door and said goodbye. As I walked away from her room, I felt a layer of myself disappear. I felt warm inside, and my heart was heavier than it had been in a while.

There's something about that woman's voice. I can close my eyes and feel the love in her words…

4:35PM

I entered the Recreation Room hoping to see all of them. Liz said they would be there, and I found myself acting as a little child, filled with whimsical anticipation. The flat-screen TV was on and CNN was tuned in. Walter sat in his wheelchair peering up at the screen, he didn't see me, and at that moment, I was okay with that. I knew he was going to be tough to win over. I quickly scanned the room, and I noticed that Liz, Cathy, and Mickey where nowhere to be found. Then I saw Kitty. She was sitting in the far corner on the sofa with something on her lap. She waved me over.

"James my darling," She began. "Come sit with me."

I paused just before I sat next to her. She was wearing a flowery-green dress, and it somehow appealed to me.

You've seen that dress before. You know you have.

"Sit…Sit with me, darling." She insisted, so I did.

Kitty was crocheting something, and beside her was a small, yet curious portable radio. The volume was low, but I could recognize the voice of Neil Diamond. Who wouldn't have?

"How are you, sweetheart?" Kitty was warm and gentle, and her smile was soul touching.

"I am doing okay." I replied. "I visited with Liz earlier today and was hoping to catch all of you down here."

"Yes, Liz told me that you visited her." Kitty began. "You're such a nice boy."

I looked into her eyes and saw such love. Kitty was the type of person you'd meet once, and never be able to forget. Her scent was pleasant and made me think of a bouquet of flowers.

"I'd love to have you visit with me." She stated. "We'd have some tea…and I'll show you my flowers…I love my flowers…do you like flowers?" Kitty was overzealous.

"Yes, I'd love to have tea with you, and I do enjoy flowers." I felt her need for company.

FLASH

The light hit me. I saw potted plants and beautiful flowers. I heard Kitty's voice—*I talk to them. Sometimes I sing to them…they grow quickly when I do.*

FLASH

"I haven't seen Mickey today. Have you?" Kitty asked. I was back on the couch with her in the Rec Room. I was moved by the vision. My emotions were racing and I felt tears build.

"No, I haven't." I started. "I will try his room when I head back upstairs."

"Oh, I know he'd be so happy to see you!" Kitty beamed, exposing her bright smile.

"Yes, Mickey seems to be a nice guy." I replied. I swallowed hard, trying to keep the tears at bay. "Last time we didn't get a chance to say much to each other."

"Oh yes," She said, placing her hand on her chest. "Walter knows how to get Mickey's goat, and they can really cause a stink."

"Are they always like that?" I asked.

Kitty giggled and repositioned herself on the couch. "Sweetheart, they are the life of the party around here." She laughed loudly. "Sometimes the girls and I look forward to their repartee." She laughed again, and her high pitch tone was almost operatic.

I couldn't control myself, so I joined in the laughter. "So do they even like each other?"

"Sweetheart, they do…they do." She took a tissue from her dress pocket and dabbed her forehead. "Under all of their fighting, I know they care about one another."

Moments later Kitty mechanically began to crochet. The conversation continued and she began to show me what she was crocheting. She mentioned that her daughter was about to give birth to their seventh child, and she knew *he* was going to be so special. She was making *him* a pillow.

FLASH

I saw *him*—The baby boy Kitty was talking about. He was held in the arms of a woman.

FLASH

My heart was beating faster and I needed to run. The flashes were sharp and vivid. Before I could get up from the couch, I was startled by Kitty, who took in a deep breath and sighed heavily. She placed the crocheting needles down on her lap, and reached for the small radio. I saw her face as she held it in her hands.

"Goodness, I love this song." She whispered. "Do you know this song, baby?"

I listened to the song and tried to make out the words. I shrugged my shoulders.

"Let me make it a bit louder." Kitty said. With her thumb, she moved the round dial.

I heard it. I heard the song. Kitty looked at me and began to sing along. It was Debbie Boone's, *You Light Up My Life*. Kitty reached out and touched my face.

FLASH

The light hit me harder and I felt myself grab the couch with my right hand. A second later, my eyes were open and I was sitting atop the mantle of an old fireplace. It was me—I was a little boy. I had to be at least seven years old. I looked down and saw my hands. They were tiny. I looked at my feet. They were also tiny and encased in Buster Brown shoes. I looked up and saw everything, except her face. In its place was a pale-pink smudge. I looked and saw her shoulders, her arms, and her hands. She was standing below me in her green dress—that green dress. I noticed a small phonograph and it was playing a forty-five. It was the song, and she was singing in harmony. Her voice was beautiful and it rang happily in my ears. Kitty sang the chorus, and then asked the little boy to sing along. I was baffled by the fact that I couldn't see her face, but it definitely was Kitty. Suddenly, I heard the voice of a young child. The voice began to sing softly, and then it began to emerge with the chorus. It was my voice. We were singing the words to the song. Kitty raised her hands and gently cupped the child's face—my face. Everything went burry and I could feel her hands lift me off the fireplace and embrace me so completely. Within her arms, I felt loved and safe— I felt at home.

FLASH

"Sweetheart, are you okay?" Kitty's troubled voice registered through the other side of the light.

I quickly passed back over and the white flash dissipated. I was in my body once again and back on the couch with Kitty. I looked at her and she could tell that something was wrong. For the second time today, I was caught in two different wormholes in time, with two individuals who should be strangers.

"James, should I call for a nurse?" Kitty was worried.

"No Kitty…I am okay…I'm fine…I'll be fine." My mouth was dry, but I managed to reassure her. I did not intend to tell her what had just happened. If I attempted, how in the world would I begin?

"Sweetheart, you look pale." Kitty put her hand on my cheek. "Do you need to rest?"

I didn't want to be rude, but I needed to leave the Rec Room—Now!

"I think you're right." I began to speak while getting up from the couch. "I should go up to my room and take it easy. It must be the meds."

Kitty reached up and took my hand. I felt the softness of her skin and in that moment, I knew we had a bond. I smiled down at her and she released my hand. I walked away and slipped through the automatic door. Today a part of me was revealed—something fresh—something new.

Kitty's laugh was a sound I remembered…God that laugh.

February 22, 2009
Sunday 10:10PM

Ian just left. He was with me most of the day, and we spent most of our time watching television. He knew something was on my mind, but I told him I needed to rest. I wanted to tell him about Liz and Kitty, but I needed to process everything. Was it the medications? What is wrong with me? Ian did not push me, instead he stayed with me, and made sure I ate and rested throughout the day. I wanted to tell him about Sarah. I wanted to confront him and demand the truth, but how in the world was I supposed to begin that conversation?

"Excuse me." Nurse Clemins walked into room. She didn't knock. "I need to check your vitals." She rolled the small cart toward my bed.

This was yet another concern. I had to find a way to sit Ian down and talk to him without worrying about a nurse barging in. I know he will listen, but even I have a hard time understanding Sarah, the dreams, and Jade. I have to wait for the right time.

"Please lift your arm." The Nurse took my blood pressure.

"I am getting tired." I informed her. Actually, I wanted her out of my room!

Nurse Clemins did not reply, but she looked down at me and rolled her eyes. She waited for the machine to finish, undid the arm cuff, placed it back into the basket, and wrote in my chart.

"Open." She directed. The digital thermometer was connected to a machine on the cart, and she forced the probe under my tongue. "I will be out of your way in ten seconds, Your Highness." She was smug and nasty.

Nurse Clemins was lucky that the probe was in my mouth, and I couldn't speak. I had a bunch of choice words for her.

FLASH

The light stuck my eyes, and then it disappeared. Nurse Clemins was still standing there.

FLASH

It happened again, and Nurse Clemins removed the thermometer probe from my mouth, and moved in closer.

"Are you okay?" She sounded concerned, but it did not last long. "Get some sleep! You look awful!"

***

Nurse Clemins left my room and slammed the door. I took a deep breath and began meditating. I used the stereo remote to turn on the system. I programmed the unit and I will sleep with the voice of Celine Dion looped on the stereo. When I hear the sound of her voice, it is as if I am listening to a lullaby. I need to put things into perspective, and there is no better way to think, while listening to the voice of an angel.

February 23, 2009
Monday 8:06 PM

Nurse Collins entered my room, with my chart in hand, at approximately 11:40 this morning. Thankfully, I was already showered and dressed. Ms. Collins informed me that I was scheduled for a battery of tests, beginning in thirty minutes. I was getting hungry and asked her if I could eat an early lunch beforehand. She apologized sharply, and told me that I would have to wait.

"Frank will be in to draw some blood." Nurse Collins stated. "Then he will take you downstairs for an eye exam, an EEG, and an MRI." She opened my chart and began to write.

She already knew I hated needles, and at my expense, it must have given her a cheap thrill to see me squirm. I tried to keep calm, but I already knew what would happen especially if I didn't have anything in my stomach. The last thing I needed was for my head to meet the cold, icy floor!

"I'll ask Frank to bring me something to eat." I exclaimed. "It's not going to happen unless I eat something."

Nurse Collins stopped writing in the chart, closed it, and then placed it under her arm. I watched her body language. Like a rattlesnake gearing up to release kinetic energy, she began to coil herself. I knew she was about to strike.

"Frank is not available!" She barked. "And, he is not your private nurse, or your maid!"

I could tell I pissed her off, and it tickled my fancy every single time. She stood there with her hand on her waist and her right toe pointed outward. It was evident that Ms. Collins reached the 'burn-out' period in her career and had as much bedside manner as a ten-day-old corpse.

"There's no reason to get your panties in a bind." I did not raise my voice. There was no reason for me to, because I already succeeded. It didn't take much to set her off. "I wouldn't ask you to get me a thing, even if you were the last friggin' nurse on the planet."

She reset her eyeglasses on her face. "Excuse me?" Nurse Collins was livid. "I'm going to report this to Doctor O'Shea. Your attitude is unacceptable!"

"Got a phone? Call the flipping Pope. Maybe, he'll give a damn." I said calmly with a smile.

It was such poetic justice, and perfect timing. Before Nurse Collins had a chance to release her venom, in walked Frank. She looked at him, shook her head, raised her arms, and then stormed out of the room.

"What was that all about?" Frank tried to be serious, but he couldn't restrain a smile. "You are awful!"

I explained everything to Frank and he said that we'd stop along the way to get a bite to eat. I asked if I had to go in the wheelchair. His facial expression said it all, and down into the wheelchair I sat. Moments later, I was on my way to the cafeteria.

12:21PM

My stomach was no longer growling. Frank waited patiently while I ate, then took me to a private room near the nurse's station. Frank did everything he could to keep my mind occupied while he drew blood. I didn't faint, but I still detested the process. He took me to get my eyes checked and then down to the basement to another exam room. He introduced me to a Doctor—a middle-age man named Vaarin Singh. Frank left us alone and said he would be back later. I sat in a recliner while the Doctor measured my head, and then drew small circles with a magic marker on my scalp. The sedative Frank administered after I ate lunch began to set in. Vaarin was forthcoming and walked me through the entire process. He mentioned that Doctor Swartz wanted to measure my brain activity while I slept. Doctor Singh continued to speak, but under the sedative, I closed my eyes and began to drift off. I heard the remnants of his voice.

...the electrodes...information to the computer...wont' feel a thing...program will...
find any abnormalities...computer will show...will take about an hour...relax...

***

The Λ Train was moving. It was travelling at average speed, and I looked around the car and noticed I was the only passenger on the train. I was back in Queens and headed somewhere toward the City. Although it was a bright and sunny day, everything felt peculiar. I stood up from my seat and carefully walked along the floor. Instinctively, I chose to make it to the first car. I had to get to the conductor. I reached out and held onto the stainless steel poll. What was I doing here? Where was I going? I had to hold on tightly because the train picked up speed. The car jolted and rocked. I moved quickly and sat down on a seat in front of the poll. I knew there was no way I was going to make it to the front car, especially if the train continued its rapid speed. Moments later, I looked outside and watched the daylight dissolve. It was swallowed by the darkness as the train took me underground. The light blinked on and off inside the car and it was evident that our speed was unsafe. I had to move—I wanted to move, but I couldn't. I remained seated but reached out and grasped the poll with both hands. The rocking and jolting increased greatly, and I did not feel it at first. Suddenly, my entire body was pulled toward the front of the train. My hands did not let go of the metal beam, and the length of my body hung horizontally in midair. The train hit something hard, and soon after, gravity was back in play. My body hit the floor abruptly, and on impulse, I crawled back toward the poll. Why were we still moving? How were we still moving? Our speed significantly decreased but the vehicle remained in motion—it felt like floating. I reached the poll and pulled myself upward. I had to blink several times before accepting what my eyes revealed. The train was underwater, and it was moving along through the underground station. I looked outside and saw the station sign for Utica Avenue. Like cemented statues, I saw them. Faceless and motionless, people stood on the platform. They were frozen in time. I quickly looked down at my feet as cold water began to drench my sneakers. Water quickly began to seep into the train from every direction.

You can control it. You can control it James. Don't be frightened.

I heard her voice echo within the car. I looked around hoping to see her, but she was not there to save me. The pressure built outside the train, and the metal-crushing sound was terrifying. I knew what was about to happen, as I looked at the window in front of me. Tiny lightning patterns appeared on its surface—they were cracking, and everything was about to implode.

Don't be scared. Find it within.

Glass shards streamed inward, and thousands of gallons of water rushed toward me. I felt the pressure suck the remaining air from the train, and all I could do was wait to drown.

Breathe…Focus…Breathe.

The water was freezing and filling the area around me. The train light blinked rapidly then immediately left me in pitch-blackness. The water was at my knees…chest…neck. It continued to creep upward until I had to hold my breath. I was now abandoned in obscurity, on the brink of death. I closed my eyes. The poll vanished from my hands, the floor left my feet, and my body began to descend.

Feel it from inside…remember…try to remember…

I sensed something in the water, and it was circling me. Was it my Harbor seal? Was it him? The water became warmer and warmer, and I opened my eyes hoping to see him. It wasn't him, but I saw them—two eyes—two balls of light. They hovered at least fifteen yards in front of me.

Focus your energy, James.

The lights came at me with immense speed, and the water around my frame continued to grow warmer.

FLASH

"James...Mr. Valvano!"

My body was back in the recliner. The room was cool and someone was yelling my name.

"Mr. Valvano!"

I opened my eyes and saw Doctor Vaarin Singh, frantically examining me, then his computer. He had the desk phone in his hand.

"James, are you okay?"

Doctor Singh mumbled something into the phone, hung it up, and then rapidly typed on the computer keyboard. My body felt fatigued, I couldn't talk, and I noticed my pants were wet. I had peed myself.

"Is he okay?" Frank bolted through the door and behind him was Doctor Swartz.

"He is awake, but he won't respond." Doctor Singh's voice was frenzied. "The readings...I don't know...He...Something has happened...I've never seen..."

"Doctor Singh!" Doctor Swartz yelled. "Stop!"

The room became silent and I rested there in the recliner. I wanted to say something, but I couldn't, and it hurt to move. Doctor Swartz asked Frank to take me back to my room, but that was the last thing I heard. The room began to spin, and my eyes fell shut. I passed out into the silence.

February 24, 2009
Tuesday 9:32 PM

It was obvious that I slept through the remainder of yesterday. I remember the vision, and of course, the wonderful feeling of sitting in my own urine. Ian was fidgeting in the chair when I woke this morning. He was eager to see me and wanted to hover. They told him about yesterday. His annoying, but predictable, actions said so. I made up a story and once again decided not to tell him the truth. I didn't have the energy. We sat around for most of the morning, but Ian had to leave for work. I remained in bed until Nurse Collins removed my lunch tray. I did not eat much. I had no appetite. I took a shower and dressed myself, then decided to visit Cathy, and Mickey. I left my room, and walked down the hall and found Cathy's room. I knocked lightly. The entire hallway was irritatingly still and quiet. I knocked again, but received no response. I moved along until I came to Mickey's room. Again, I knocked lightly and waited. There was no sound from inside.

They are either sleeping or downstairs in the Recreation Room.

Before I made it back to my room, I heard a door creak open. I turned around and saw Liz at her door. She was still dressed in her nightgown.

"James." She said my name, and I could tell something was awry in the tone of her voice.

I walked toward her, and I noticed she had been crying.

"Liz, are you okay? I hope I didn't bother you." I felt guilty for waking her.

"No honey, you didn't bother me. I heard someone knocking out here, and I figured it was you." She had a tissue in her hand and wiped her eyes."

"Liz, what's wrong? Are you sick?" I was worried.

"No honey. You didn't hear the awful news?" She sounded distraught.

"No, what happened?" At that moment, I was not ready to hear any bad news.

"It's a tragedy…It's just dreadful." She began to sob. "They transferred Cathy to another facility this morning, and no one will tell me where she is."

"That's ridiculous." I saw her pain. I could see in her eyes just how lost she was.

"Honey it gets worse." Liz started to sob harder. "Nurse Collins went to give Kitty her medication, and found Kitty…Kitty passed away."

I felt a burning sensation within my stomach and my heart sank.

"Liz, I'm so sorry." I put my arms around her and let her cry. I held her tightly and my heart broke into pieces. I closed my eyes and wished I could take away her pain.

I actually felt a sensation of loss. My stomach continued to ache and my heart pounded on end.

"Liz, it will be okay." I tried to say something to calm her. We ended our hug and I looked into her eyes. "Kitty is in a better place, and as for Cathy, we'll find out where and why they transferred her."

Liz wiped away her tears and I saw how weak she was.

"Let me help you back into bed…please just rest." I walked with her and held her close.

FLASH

White light glazed my eyes. I felt Liz in my grasp, and I looked over at the piano. Water began to flow from the picture frames, and then down to the floor. The space filled with sounds of crying people. Were the cries coming from her relatives? The water continued to rush toward our feet, and I had only one reaction—to protect Liz. The smell of saltwater and rotting kelp filled my nostrils.

FLASH

I was still walking alongside Liz, and had my arm across her back. I searched for the water, but the room was dry. The picture frames were resting calmly on top of the piano, and our voices were the only sounds inside the room.

"Thank you James. You are such a good man." Liz was drained and her voice was almost lifeless.

I helped her into her bed. "I want you to get some sleep, Liz. I will make sure you are okay."

I placed the comforter over her tired body, and ran my fingers through her hair. Liz closed her eyes, and slowly fell into a deep sleep. Before I left her side, I kissed her gently on her forehead. I loved her and had to protect her. I looked over at her family, as they remained timelessly held inside varied frames.

"...we will be okay...all of us...I promise."

February 27, 2009
Friday 10:30 PM

I was sickened! I told the nurses that I was concerned about Liz, and hoped they would make sure she was looked after. Since Wednesday morning, I tried to visit Liz, but the staff told me that she was sedated, and no visits were permitted. I was so depressed and angry today. I realized that it no longer mattered. This place was not a hospital! It was a prison! I paced my room for almost an hour, and my legs felt the stress and fatigue. I entered the bathroom, and quickly shed my clothing. I stood naked, looking at myself in the bathroom mirror, examining every flaw. The tears continued to fall, and I remained focused on my receding hairline, and the white beginning to show itself from my goatee. My skin was pale, and the dark circles under my eyes made me feel like a monster—the living dead. I wanted to be twenty-one again. I no longer wanted to be inside this body.

You will be alone! You are going to die alone!

I might as well be alone, considering I feel alone every day. I am locked up in here like a dirty secret. I wanted it to stop! I needed the pain, the anger, and the fear to stop. I wanted, and most of all, needed to know the truth.

It is inside. The truth is within. Search for it. You will find me there.

Tick…Tick…Jerk

I continued to observe myself in the mirror, and hated the uncontrollable movements. I no longer owned the right side of my body. It had become a foreign part of me; a part of me I loathed. The man in the mirror was lonely, ugly, and unworthy.

Today I chose to be alone. I sat most of the day looking out my window. I am feeling emotionally, mentally, and physically drained. I am so lost. I listened to every single Celine Dion CD and tried to purge the negativity. However, today it was not working. I can tell they increased the level of medications. I have become empty, desensitized, and detached. Ian visits almost every day but there are days I wished he didn't. Some days I didn't care. Today I wrote a letter to Dr. O'Shea, and asked Frank to deliver it to her. I couldn't deal with a session this morning, so instead I decided to write what I was feeling. I haven't been able to speak candidly with Ian yet, but I know I have to soon. I want to tell him everything. I want to hear the words come from my own mouth. I don't want him to think I am insane, but he is all I have. Everyone else has abandoned me!

What if there's a camera in this room? In my bedroom? Sarah may be right!

These thoughts constantly travelled through my mind. Was I being paranoid for no reason? Maybe I should stop taking the medications.

Worry about finding a way to gain access to Doctor O'Shea's office!

I want to read Doctor O'Shea's notes, and look through my file. I have to talk with Sarah again! She just might know a way to get what I need. I have nothing to lose, and will do whatever it takes to get out of this place. I heard her voice calling…

James, be careful! You know what must be done!

March 3, 2009
Tuesday 11:45 PM

The medications continued to arrive three times a day, and my sleep pattern was erratic. *They* said that it was expected, and to give my body additional time to adjust. I still had not seen Liz, and no one will tell me what happened to Cathy. The entire situation angers me, but the only thing I can do is wait. Today I spent a great deal of time thinking about my brother John. I wondered how he was doing. I thought back to the past, and replayed those days repeatedly in my head. I moved to Florida in 1993, and four years later, my family decided to do the same. They left New York behind and chose to roll the dice on a new life. John was the only sibling who decided to remain in New York. He continued to live his life independently and no one was the wiser. We had no clue what was coming. As time went by, John had gotten into a couple of car accidents and we marked it up to the consequences of living in the Big Apple. Four years later, my parents drove up the coast to help him pack and escorted him down to Florida. We had no clue, but each day he became unrecognizable. Did he have a stroke? Were the car accidents relative or responsible for what we were witnessing? He was simply not our brother. Something was wrong with him. Time went by and we urged him to seek medical attention. Regardless of our concerns and requests, John protested. It began to worsen quickly—rapidly. John continued to drive his vehicle even though we urged him not to. The day came. The day of his final car accident, which put a stop to his driving, and inevitably, it put into motion his downward spiral. John moved in with my parents and they suffered along with him. His motor skills were abnormal, however it did not compare to the emotional and psychological tribulations he, and the entire family were facing. What was this? What do we do? It was painful and so intensely frustrating. His outbursts and rants pained my parents, but John finally submitted and agreed to seek medical attention. After a multitude of testing, the hospital established that John was suffering from a vitamin-B12 deficiency. There had to be more! Could he have Parkinson's disease? Thankfully, my parents did not give up. They took him to seek the advice of a neurologist. It was clear. After a single test result, he was diagnosed with this life-altering, life-stealing, unforgiving disease. He was once an independent, successful businessperson, and a professional dancer, as well as instructor. He and my mother used to win contests at the local dance studio in Queens, and John had a huge network of friends, and girlfriends. None of us would have ever guessed that this individual—our brother—would now be degrading in a group home, knocking on death's door.

I will not be like him!

The visits to the group home were bittersweet, heartbreaking, emotional, and so draining. Each time I left, a piece of me died. However, it was more important to see John happy, and safe. I worked with individuals with developmental disabilities for over ten years. It felt so rewarding to help those who were in need. I attended many Special Olympic outings, worked for group homes, managed one, and then decided to leave the field. I never looked back. However, here I sit; a resident of a facility similar to the ones I worked for. Irony?

I know I have to accept what has happened. Each day is a battle with this disease. It shattered and broke John, and brought me to this cold and far away facility. I want to escape. I want to feel the warmth of the sun. I want to be held by the ocean. I want to disappear into the world underneath the sea. I just want someone to love all of this away…someone.

Where are you Jade?

The Struggle, Back to Me
Oh the noise…The profound finality from within my head.
Please do not take the best of me—I want to share it so completely.
Oh the pain, the struggle from within my heart,
The overflow of such anger, rages from within my broken soul.
Oh the hellish anxiety, barring me from what I know is true.
I fear not death's door, but the timing is profoundly too soon.
Oh, the mirror I stand before is no friend, no friend to its own reflection.
How ugly I must be for it to deny me my own appearance.
I insist—I demand to see it—my heart held in another's grasp.
Oh the sadness, my eyes are incessantly blinded by the tears.
I am losing strength…I am losing ground…The glass sits almost empty.
Oh, the struggle back to me seems futile at best—I must submit. The end
is already written, so I must journey along until I vanish.
The struggle back to me—The struggle.

March 5, 2009
Thursday 9:56PM

I heard a noise outside my bedroom door. I didn't know what it was, but something was outside in the hall. CNN was on the TV, and the sound was barely audible. I quickly put on my workout shorts, a T-shirt, and then headed toward the door. Without hesitation, I opened the door and headed into the hallway. The corridor was vaguely lit by the three evenly separated, hanging light fixtures. I strained my eyes to see down the entire floor. She stood there. A woman in a dark robe stood with her back facing the length of the hallway.

"Hello?" I called out. "Are you okay?"

She turned and began to walk toward me. I barely felt it, but the hallway began to rock slowly. Her pace turned into a sprint, and she tried to make it toward me without falling.

"We are going to drown! We are going to drown!" She was shouting. She swerved from one side of the hall to the other.

I heard the elevator open behind her, and a tidal wave of water entered the hall. She and the water came rushing forward, and I remained caught in terror. My body could not move, and she and the rogue wave were barreling toward me.

FLASH
Do you remember? This was another time…

I heard Jade's voice in the distance. I was scared; however, I knew another transformation was taking place. I could not stop it from happening.

The illumination stung me, and when I regained my eyesight, I was standing on the deck of a huge ship. The woman was dressed in a luxurious rose-colored Edwardian gown, and her hair was drawn tightly—Pompadour style. She held my hands tightly, and her eyes were filled with tears.

"My love, we are going to drown! They said we hit something very hard!" The woman's voice was of a regional English dialect.

FLASH

"My darling, I love you." I let go of her hand as she was helped into a lifeboat.

FLASH

The ship buckled and broke apart. I felt my body enter the frigid, black water. I slipped under, and saw the bodies. Hundreds of bodies were drifting downward—lifeless. I decided to surrender to the inevitable, and then suddenly I saw the tiny flickering light. It zipped below me, and then swirled around my body. The water temperature began to rise near and around me, however I could not hold my breath any longer. The animated ball of light came upon me, and captured my body. I felt the sensation, and it felt like being turned inside out.

FLASH

The altered-state dissolved, and I stood outside my bedroom, staring down the hallway. Nothing was moving, and no one was there. I heard the elevator door open, and moments later the doors closed. I entered my room and resumed the one position I became accustomed to lately—staring up at the ceiling.

March 6, 2009
Friday 10:11PM

Today, Doctor O'Shea was sitting at her desk when I walked into the room. I did not use the walker, or the wheelchair. I asked Frank not to escort me today, so he remained at the nurse's station down the hall.

"Good morning." I opened the conversation. Last night's hallucination remained fresh in my mind, but I did everything I could to stay focused.

"Yes, good morning, James." She returned.

I knew Doctor O'Shea was about to commence our session, so I decided to talk first.

"I owe you an apology." I began. "My behavior and the way I spoke to you in our last meeting were inappropriate." I had to change it up and begin to play nice.

"James, we need to move forward and continue to take things slowly." She sounded very diplomatic, and sincere. She then took out the tape recorder and began recording.

Jerk...Tick

"I also apologize for missing our last meeting. I sent you the letter to explain how I was feeling." I stated.

"That was a proactive decision, one I was pleased to see." Doctor O'Shea noted.

I hoped this meeting would go smoothly and truly wanted to find some reason to trust her. After the incident with Sarah, I grew more weary and mistrusting of the staff. I continued to struggle with these feelings, and I did not yet have a chance to talk to Ian.

"I want to go over the past two weeks. I would like to comment on your letter, then I will address the nurse's and Tonya's PT reports." She declared.

She opened my letter, and I noticed red marks on several sentences.

She dove right in. "You claim that our meetings are unproductive because you feel I am trying to trap you or cause you to become angry." She looked at me. "Can you explain what you mean?"

Jerk...Jerk

"Well, at times you make it very uncomfortable and it truly makes me uneasy. It almost feels like sitting with the principal in grade school." I laid it out there for her.

"James, it is my responsibility to make sure that your mental, physical, and emotional health improves." She started. "Sometimes you may not like to hear what I have to say, or how I position the questions. Ultimately, everything is your choice. I cannot change you, and I cannot make you think or feel a certain way. My goal with each of my patients is to help them find their own inner strengths and live life to their fullest potential."

Tick...Tick

"Another part of your letter concerns me." She claimed. "You specifically mentioned life would not be worth living if the disease progressed as it did in your brother's case." She put the letter down and sat back in her chair. "Let's address this. Can you explain why you feel this way?"

We sat there for several seconds. I looked at her and wanted to make myself clear.

"Can I ask you a question first?" I began to position my thoughts.

"Yes you may, absolutely." She permitted.

"Here's a scenario. Imagine you were diagnosed with this disease. You have the physical abnormalities. You slowly forget things and become very clumsy. You battle with depression, anxiety, and experience moments of anger and confusion. You are placed on several medications that screw with your system. You know there is no cure, the progression will happen, and you will die from this disease. How would you feel?"

Dr. O'Shea took several moments. She made a few notes then returned to her position in her chair.

Jerk...Tick...Tick

"James, you bring up a key question." She paused. "Truly, I do not know how I would react. As a Doctor—a psychiatrist, I fervently reflect on my own humanity. Since the day I spoke with my first patient, I quickly recognized that it could be quite frustrating from this side of the desk. So never forget that I am human, also."

"Can you see why I feel the way I do?" I replied.

"Without question James, however I have to ensure each of my patients are receiving the preeminent, and proper treatment. It is my responsibility to guarantee your safety, and the safety of each of the patients here at CNS." Doctor O'Shea verbalized her professional mission.

Jerk...Tick...Tick

I remained quiet. I did not want to cause any flux. I had to continue to be on my best behavior.

"Honestly speaking, James." She broke the lull. "I want you to understand what can manifest from having this disease."

Tick...Tick

Doctor O'Shea began to speak. She began to explain everything I already knew about the disease. I saw her lips moving, but I shut her out. I began to daydream. I felt the warm sun on my shoulders. I wanted nothing more than to dig my toes into the sand and wait for the ocean to touch me with its consuming arms. I wanted to see my seal. I wanted to understand the connection. I wanted to know why *they* chose me. Why did Jade choose me?

"James, are you listening to me?" Doctor O'Shea broke my daydream.

I noticed that she had been looking through my file. She began to readdress my medical history, yet again.

"James, your medical history indicates years of depression, anxiety, and social withdrawal. It also indicates behavioral abnormalities such as irrational anger and inappropriate fits of rage. For the record, Ian made mention of a few issues. With concern, he made me aware that he noticed the physical abnormalities for at least ten years. In the beginning, the involuntary movements were infrequent, but as time went on, he saw the progression. The rage and anger came later on…"

I sat there listening to her. I could not deny anything. I detested being placed under a microscope, and it was hard to hear the truth, especially from a stranger. In my eyes she was still a stranger, nevertheless, I had no choice but to listen and realize that Ian told her everything. Ian told her about our most private moments—the most difficult moments.

Why would he betray me?

She continued to illustrate each single thing wrong with me. "Ian told me that there was a time you tried to attack him. He also stated that over a ten-year period he witnessed you become incessantly jealous and accusatory. Just before your accident, he noticed that you dropped things more frequently, you became more forgetful, and your mood swings were more regular." Doctor O'Shea stopped and looked at me.

Jerk…Tick…Tick

"I will not deny any of that." I stated. It was the truth, and I had to suck it up and account for it.

"Many individuals who suffer from this disease show the same behavior. Some even try to commit suicide. Some unfortunately succeed." She gathered.

Once again, I did not say a word. I sat there and looked at her.

James, I am here. Relax, and think of the water…

Each time I heard her voice, it was so intoxicating. She always knew when I needed her. All I wanted was for Jade to make things clear. I wanted to know what to do.

"Tonya continues to report that you are getting stronger each day." Doctor O'Shea moved on. The topic of suicide was quickly left in the past. "Tonya noted that each physical therapy session is productive. She will create a weekly schedule for you to use the hydrotherapy tub and lap pool. I will allow her to begin these sessions at her own discretion."

Doctor O'Shea continued to read the reports aloud. "The nurse's reports have not changed. The assessments continue to express negative, and inappropriate behavior, as well as noncompliance. Once again, Frank's reports lack such claims. I know you have a good relationship with Frank, however I would like you to try with the other nurses."

Tick…Jerk

I knew better than to revisit my demands from our last session, but I had to speak my mind.

"Doctor O'Shea." I caught her attention. "Will you allow Ian to bring me a few books, my laptop, and can I see my cats?" Although these requests from our last session seemed inconsequential, I truly wanted each of them. All of it was important to me. Even if she didn't allow the computer, I longed to see my cats. Dusk and Caesar were such an important part of my life, and it took a long time to get used to not seeing them. Being separated from them made me understand how a parent would feel, if separated from their children. At times, a picture is only a picture. I wanted to hold my babies. I wanted to reconnect with them.

She put the folder down and sat back in her chair. "Ian may bring you reading material, which I will approve, however I will not permit the laptop and visits with your animals." She was unwavering.

"Fine. Not a problem." I mumbled. She had no idea how deeply she just hurt me.

I will never forgive you! You are an insensitive bitch!

She sat there on her pedestal, full of herself. She looked triumphant, and untouchable. With her claws, Doctor O'Shea reached for the phone and called the nurse's station.

Jerk...Tick...Tick

I waited for her to hang up the phone. I wanted to mention a few things to her before leaving. At this point, I had nothing to lose.

"I would like to have more interaction with the other patients in this wing. Will that be a problem?" She had to see the tears building in my eyes.

Tick...Tick

"With whom?" She asked.

"You know who they are." I retorted. "I told you I already met them. You transferred Cathy somewhere and Kitty just recently passed away. Mickey, Walter and Liz are the only ones left." I wanted her to respond but she did not. "Thank God I was there to comfort Liz when she needed someone, but for some reason, I am not allowed to see her right now."

Doctor O'Shea was processing my request. Sometimes it felt as if I were talking to a fast food, drive-through box. I didn't give her a chance to respond.

"I thought it would be healthy for us to mingle. Have you ever held group sessions? I think that would be helpful, and we could probably learn a lot from each other."

She continued to sit there. Was I not speaking? Did I suggest something so outrageous?

You could never trust her! You need to listen to Sarah!

"I will take that into consideration." She finally broke her silence. "Like I said, we need to take this time to focus on your rehabilitation. It is crucial that I limit any amount of social stimulation."

"Whatever you say Doc, you know what's best for me." I surrendered. The tears were falling. I felt broken—unfixable.

I stood up and began to walk out of her office. I heard Frank coming down the small hallway.

"I will see you next week James." Doctor O'Shea uttered.

Frank met me in the corridor and we headed toward the elevator. He saw my pain. He saw the tears. He put his arm around me and I cried. I cried hard. I was mad as hell!

March 9, 2009
Monday 11:22PM

I made sure she was gone before I jumped out of bed. I switched the lights on. About fifteen minutes ago, Sarah woke me from a deep sleep. I heard her feet as she dragged them along the carpet. She stopped at the foot of my bed and started mumbling. I thought she was sleepwalking because her words were incoherent. She stood at the foot of my bed. The light from the television bathed her body and I was unable to see her face. Sarah had a difficult time standing still. She rocked from one side to the other. Her hands were at her side, and she began to mumble something once again.

"...sssshee issss gooooinnngg toooo killllllll ussssssssssss...sssssheee issss gooooinnngg toooo killllllll ussssssssssss...sssshee issss gooooinnngg toooo killllllll ussssssssssss..."

I remained as still as possible under the covers, but her entire physical and verbal presentation terrified me. I watched as she continued to sway slowly from one side, then to the other. Her swing was creepy and part of me wanted to scream, just to wake her. However, the last thing anyone could do was predict how Sarah would react. I wished I had a baseball bat nearby, or in my hands!

"...I willllllllllll kiiiillllllll...I willllllllllll kiiiillllllll...Alllll offff youuuuuu..."

I waited and waited. I hoped she would wake up, or just walk out! Without warning, she stopped swaying and stood motionless at my feet.

She pointed at me, and her voice jarred the room. "You have to tell him! He has to help us!"

My heart was now in my throat, and I was paralyzed. Again, she started to rock from one side to the other. Moments later, she began to turn and walk toward the door. I remained silent and watched her leave the room, her body bobbling from side to side. Sarah slammed the door behind her.

I have to tell Ian before it is too late.

James, you must choose to see the truth...

March 10, 2009
Tuesday 9:07PM

My body was weak and everything seemed wrong from the moment I opened my eyes this morning. The feeling lingered on throughout the day, and I knew it as soon as I entered the gym this evening for my physical therapy session. Any amount of PT was a big mistake. I was weak, distracted, and very depressed. The last several days were very challenging. I felt dizzy, lightheaded, and sleepy most of the day, but continued PT each night. At times, an unsettling calm would come upon me, and I made sure to report everything to the nurses. Frank, Ian, and Tonya were the only ones worried, and took time to watch over me during PT. It was just a matter of time. If Doctor O'Shea's goal was to design a zombie, she had definitely succeeded. She upped my medications again this week, and the result of her professional medical decision literally hit the floor in the gym this evening.

I had been working on the leg press machine for at least fifteen minutes. I decided to stop, as the room slowly began to vanish. I began to sweat profusely, and my body felt cold and heavy. I stood up slowly from the machine and turned toward Tonya. She noticed it from several feet away and rushed toward me. No one was in reach, and down I went. Like a falling tree, I hit the floor hard.

I woke sharply to a horrendous smell. It was indeed smelling-salt.

One of the nurses had me propped up and as I opened my eyes, I saw the crowd. In the background, I heard Ian yelling at Doctor O'Shea. Ian was enraged, and without reserve, he vocalized it for everyone to hear. It was so sweet to hear him lay into her. It almost made fainting, worthwhile. I was lucky, as the majority of my upper body came down on a blue mat. I escaped broken bones, and only suffered a few bruises, and a dose of embarrassment. Abruptly, Ian and Frank parted the circle of staff, and came to my side. Moments later Doctor Swartz joined Ian and Frank.

Doctor Swartz looked me over and agreed that I was lucky to have fallen on the mat. Tonya came rushing over from her office with a spare wheelchair. I could tell Ian was beyond his breaking point. Frank and Tonya helped me off the mat and into the wheelchair. Ian put his hand on my head, looked at Frank, and asked him to take me back to my room. Frank did not protest. Before we exited through the automatic doors, I heard Ian demand a meeting with both doctors.

"Oh my God." Frank mumbled. "Ian is going to take their heads off."

"It doesn't matter. I will be going home soon." I whispered.

Frank did not respond. He continued to steer the wheelchair. I closed my eyes and imagined the sun on my skin. I envisioned the sand beneath my feet and the rushing waves. I wanted to go…into the water…down beneath the waves. I will have to wait until she takes me again. I want to see it. I want to see it all—everything!

It was just after nine o'clock when Ian entered my room. Nurse Clemins left moments ago after quickly administering meds. Ian noticed the room was silent, and I was propped up in bed. He knew I was waiting for him. I wanted to know what he said to Doctor "Pill-Pusher".

"So, tell me how it went." I eagerly wanted to know.

Ian brought over a chair and sat beside my bed.

"I should have called for this meeting a while ago." Ian seemed tired. He put his hands on his face and rubbed his eyes. "Frank and Tonya noticed the change in you, and we should have known better."

Ian took a moment and shifted his body in the chair until he became comfortable. I could tell that he had so much weighing him down. I could see that he was tired.

"They should have given you time to adjust to the meds. You could have hurt yourself tonight." Ian spoke softly. "You won't have to worry about PT until you adjust to the meds."

Tick...Jerk

"Thank you for meeting with the doctors." I felt assured.

Was it the right time to ask Ian another round of questions? I held off for so long, but now we were alone, and I wanted answers.

"Ian, I need to talk to you. I don't want you to think I'm crazy."

Ian sat back in the chair and put his feet up on the bed.

"Go ahead." He replied.

"I want you to be honest with me, no matter what." I looked into his eyes.

Ian nodded his head and waited for me to speak. I took a few moments and blurted it out.

"If I wanted to leave this place, could you make that decision? Could we just pack my things and sign out?"

Ian took a few moments, and from the look on his face, I knew I was not going to like what he had to say.

"James, it's complicated. Let me explain our situation. When I chose to bring you here there was so much going on, and I already explained to you that coming here was our only option. You know our financial situation, and it hasn't gotten any better. Without medical benefits, we had very few options. That hasn't changed either."

I interrupted him. "So are you saying I can't leave?"

"It's not that easy." Ian started again. "I would like nothing more than to bring you home."

Tick...Tick...Jerk

"Then what's the problem? I'm no longer in a coma, or in a wheelchair." I stated.

"No one is happier than me to see you out of the coma and able to walk. That isn't the point."

Tick...Jerk

"Ian, are you telling me that I have to stay here?" I asked him.

"No, I am saying that you need to stay here. I know you don't like it here, and you don't feel comfortable with Doctor O'Shea, but I want you to receive the best possible treatment."

I did not expect to hear this from Ian. My heart sunk and the one person I could always count on wanted me to remain in this prison. He was going to make me rot here!

You cannot trust anyone, not even Ian!

"I thought you were going to tell me that we were leaving, especially after what happened tonight. I heard how angry you were in the gym." I began to feel anxious.

"Yes, I was angry about their decision to continue with physical therapy, especially because I saw what the medications were doing to you."

Tick...Tick

I began to think. Was Sarah right? Was Ian not telling me the whole truth? It was now up to me and me alone. I had to work on a plan to get out of here! First, I had to get into Doctor O'Shea's office. I had to find out about the others. I was more concerned for Liz. She was helpless. I had to help all of them. Regardless, I had to find out the truth.

"James, we can't give up. We have to hope the medications will eventually stop the tremors. I know you want that."

I listened to Ian, but an icy calm crept up my body, and cloaked me once again. The medications slowly made their way through my body, like a python slithering down a tree. I hated it. I loved it. I didn't want it. I had to have it. I felt no control, and soon, my body was calm.

Ian would never lie, would he? I don't understand.

"James, you know they can only treat the symptoms of the disease. I will never let anything happen to you."

I wonder if it's still snowing outside.

"You have to trust me James. I will be here with you no matter what. I want you to be healthy, mentally and physically."

Is it time for my medication? How about a nice walk...

"James, you are so important to me...to our family. We all love you...we all want you to come home."

I have to play nice. I have to play nice.

I looked at Ian. Through glossy, heavy, and drugged eyes, I looked at him.

"I understand Ian. I know you are just looking out for me, and I will do whatever it takes to get out of this place."

I wonder if it's snowing outside.

"I don't want you to stress yourself." Ian stood up. "Please get some sleep and relax. It's been a rough evening."

Smile at him! Smile at the traitor!

"I'll be fine, just fine." I replied, and followed with a smile.

"I'll see you after work. I am going to bring you a bunch of books, and maybe a chocolate ice cream sundae with loads of hot fudge and chocolate sprinkles." Ian's voice was still inside the room.

I felt a hand on my head. Maybe it was his hand.

"Everything will be okay." The voice stated.

"Thank you." I casually mentioned.

Moments later I heard the door close. I remained propped up in the bed all alone. I allowed the evil medications to take over my soul. I sit here with you. I want to tear you to pieces. My precious journal, shall I introduce you to fire? I have to do more than play nice with the Staff. I must put on a performance of a lifetime. One performance this place has never seen! I heard Jade's voice invade the room.

James, do not give up! You are stronger…you must fight it…

March 13, 2009
Friday 9:52PM

It happened again today—another vision, another flash. I waited in Doctor O'Shea's office. Frank mentioned that she was running late, so I decided to sit by her window and wait for her arrival. It was a bit windy outside in the courtyard. I watched the trees sway and lean gently as the seasonal winds passed through. It has been such a long time since I felt the breeze against my face, and I closed my eyes to recall those days. I remembered how it was to smell the flowers—Jasmine, Freesias, Gardenias, and the Roses!

FLASH

"Damn it! Be careful! Come down from there!" A woman's voice penetrated through the white light.

I opened my eyes and we were high upon a cliff with a range of mountains in the distance. I looked down at my body—at my feet, legs, and my hands. I was in my mid teens.

"This isn't funny Walter!" The woman cried out into the canyon.

Walter? How could it be? He was younger—probably in his late fifties. Nevertheless, it was Walter. Without a wheelchair, and an oxygen mask, Walter was in my vision. He had climbed out onto a tree, which was growing over the edge, off the cliff. Another voice cried out into the distance; however, I could not see anyone other than Walter. The other's faces were unrevealing, but their voices were recognizable.

"Don't mess around! Get back here!" It was a woman, and she stood beside me.

Suddenly, another man jumped onto the tree and joined Walter. Walter, and now this man, laughed at the women's fears. They joked with them, and continued to taunt them. They were playing, but within this vision, I felt my heart heavy with nerves. I, too, was worried for their lives. Walter and the other man finally came down from the tree and back to safety. I tried again to see their faces, but Walter's was the only one this delusion allowed. Quickly, he moved toward me. Walter pointed his finger at me, winked, and then said I was a good kid. He patted me on the back and said that he loved me. I felt a connection, but it happened way too fast.

FLASH

"Good morning James. James?" Doctor O'Shea's voice shattered the vision, and following her intrusion, I heard her place the tape recorder down upon her desk.

I turned toward her and got up from the chair. "Good morning." I responded, and made my way to the seat by her desk.

"Is everything okay?" Doctor O'Shea inquired. She was already seated at her desk, with her pen in hand.

"Yes, I was just daydreaming. It looks beautiful outside."

The Doctor made no comment about the weather. She chose to stay far away from any and every topic regarding the word—'outside'.

"How are you sleeping?" She asked.

Was I going to tell her the truth? Absolutely not! "I am sleeping much better now. I believe I am getting used to the medications."

"That's good to hear." She responded, and then opened the bottom draw of her desk. "I want to try something different today."

Doctor O'Shea took out a blank sheet of typing paper and handed it to me. She turned toward her briefcase and searched for something inside it.

What is she up to, now?

The Doctor pulled her hand from the briefcase and handed me a box of crayons.

"James, I want you to draw me a road." She began. "Take your time. I want you to imagine a road, and then draw it."

I didn't have the energy to question her, nor did I want to get into an argument. I noticed that she was a bit shocked that I didn't question her motives. I took the crayons and began to draw.

I pictured myself walking down to the beach. As soon as I took the last step off the boardwalk, I felt the sand warm beneath my bare feet. Therefore, I colored. The sand was so white and powdery. The path however, was not straight; instead, it bent toward the left, cutting through rich green foliage. Therefore, I colored. I could not capture the sounds, or the smells, but it did not matter. Then, the undergrowth, and shrubbery began to minimize. Therefore, I colored. I heard the calling waves—and that too, I could not express in tangible color tones. I removed three shades from the box to blend the end of my road—the ocean itself, full of waves and foam. Then, high in the distance I portrayed a deep orange sun, as it began to rise from the sea. She asked me to draw my road, and so I did.

"Here." I said, holding the colored sheet out in front of Doctor O'Shea.

She took it and looked at it for several seconds. "Thank you James." She placed the crayoned picture into my folder. "That will be all for today."

I thought I misunderstood the Doctor, but she in fact said that we were done.

"You can head back to your room or wherever you wish." She declared. "I will see you next week."

I didn't ask any questions. I remained calm and left the room at an even pace. After closing the door to her office, I entered the hallway in a confused haze.

What was she planning?

March 21, 2009
Saturday 10:16 PM

Tonya keeps telling me that I am getting stronger by the day. I am doing everything I can to adhere to our agreed training schedule. I meditate more often and I am trying to focus on the positive. It isn't easy. Tonya deals with me when I am having a bad day, although I probably deserve a good serving of what I give! Ian continues to be supportive and sometimes he attends my PT, and weight-training sessions. I overheard Ian and Tonya talking earlier today. I was about to walk into her office to check-off my daily activities, but Ian was there, obviously in a private, pre-planned meeting.

"I am worried about him." Ian began. "You are monitoring him while he lifts weights, right?" Sometimes even Ian could be a bit tenacious and rude when it came to me.

Of course, Tonya understood Ian's concerns. She put him at ease, and in detail, went over my entire weight-training regimen.

"He is stronger than he knows." Tonya underscored. "Everything will be okay."

I left before either of them knew I was standing outside her office. As I took the elevator up to my floor and walked to my room, I thought about how it would feel to be outside. I missed the fresh air. I missed lying out in the sun. I missed the sounds of my nieces and nephews—their laughter. I missed my family. I longed for it all. I missed it all.

I missed my home in Florida. I will lay here tonight and think of everyone and the life I used to lead.

March 24, 2009
Tuesday 11:01 PM

The dream—the revelation, was extraordinary, and unimaginable. It began with a humming sound. I was fast asleep in my bed, and the sound filled my ears. I heard her voice—Jade's breathtaking voice.

This was a time of great importance to you. You lived among them and among us...

FLASH

A young boy stood looking up at me. At first, his appearance was stranger than the words coming from his mouth. I looked at his face, and found myself studying him. His skin was oiled, and his eyes were meticulously painted and exemplified with a dark shade of eyeliner. His baldhead was apparent, and his body was covered in a white Shenti, pleated with gold thread. His feet adorned leather sandals. He spoke again, his words still incomprehensible, but persistent. He touched my arm.

FLASH

It hit me again, the swift white light. His words entered my ears and they registered.

"Father, we are approaching." The boy's voice was aimed toward me, and I fell into his ancient eyes. "Look, Father."

Everything was entering my view. The moment of confusion was clearing, and my body felt a slow, but steady drift. I was on a boat with this boy—a boy I had never seen before—the boy who called me Father. The boat, which was about eight meters long, was constructed of bunched papyrus reeds, which were braced and secured with twined lashings. Ten faceless men rowed the vessel down the river, five on one side, and five on the other. With paddles in hand, they moved in tandem.

"Father, look..." The boy urged me to turn toward the bow. He removed his hand from my forearm.

We were a part of you then, and now...

Jade whispered into my ears, and I turned to see the most sensational view. The configuration was coming up on our side, and I caught a beam of light as it soared across the expanse. I watched it shoot upward and out of view into the clouds. Horizontally, above each of the three zeniths, random translucent objects hovered in place. The megalithic, triangular structures were covered in gold, and thousands of chanting people knelt before their bases. The three formations glimmered so brightly, and in the distance, I heard what sounded like the cry of a whale. I felt it coming, and just before the white flash of light bombarded my eyes, an astronomical flying machine came down from the clouds. Its shape was triangular—not stone, but completely machine. It opened its hull, and I watched in amazement as it placed the half-lion, half-human structure in place. Once it completed its task, it shot upward and vanished. The metal discs joined the floating glass orbs, and they hovered for several moments over the structures. Then, they jetted outward. The metal ships disappeared into the sky, while the glass orbs dove into the river around us.

It was part of your path, but you are not ready yet...

FLASH

My body rested on the mattress. The flash woke me suddenly, and I remained motionless peering up at the ceiling. I have no clue what these visions are, but they are moving, and realistic. I will continue to welcome them. I will continue to wonder.

Jade, what are you trying to tell me?

March 26, 2009
Sunday 10:22 PM

Will Ian think I am crazy? Will he come back and visit me if I open up and tell him everything? I would never think of discussing it with Doctor O'Shea. The single consolation of being here at CNS was Jade. There are things I cannot explain. There are questions, many questions. The dreams are starting to change, and grow. Most of the time while I am *there*, my body is enclosed within some type of protective glass bubble. A force of an unknown kind pulls me along through the most beautiful reefs and open crevasses. If I close my eyes and concentrate, I can still hear the faint sound of its motor. It was unlike any motor I had ever heard. It hums. It barely vibrates. This glass bubble resembles a small, single passenger mini-submarine. There are no buttons, no wires, no controls, and no seats. Once inside the sphere, I am sitting, but it feels like it is a part of my body—part of my outer shell. I remember feeling amazed by the perfect view, untainted by the shape of the glass orb. The machine was seamless and unbelievably perfect in every way. In each event, within each reverie, Surgeonfish, Damselfish, and beautiful colonies of Anthias swam alongside. Beneath the glass, I witnessed the ever-changing depth of the topography below. Dolphins often came into view, and I noticed that the submergible always followed their path. While it moved my body through the water, it offered an unattainable view of marine life of every kind, shape, size, and color. I witnessed the exquisite authority of natures design. Immeasurable and rugged seawalls were saturated with life, until blue became the unvarying color as we dove into deeper waters. I can still feel the invigorating anticipation I experienced while there, under the sea. One second the sphere would move me slowly through the current, then instantly, it would soar with such bizarre speeds. Although I enjoyed the peaceful and wondrous adventure, deep inside I always hoped to see him—my seal. Lately, these dreams would end so unexpectedly. However, just before my spirit would reenter my body, the ball would drop to incredible depths. I would capture a glimpse of a brilliant light in the distance. It was beautiful. It was calling me. Part of me yearned for the light, and another could not shake the sense of apprehension. Was it fear, or was it just the unknowing? Ultimately, I wanted to experience it. I wanted Jade to explain it all to me. As each day passes, I remain eager to hear her voice. Honestly, nothing else keeps me breathing, but the thought of her return, and the notion that one day all of this will make sense. I will be ready.

April 5, 2009
Early Sunday Morning—5:14AM

I could not wait. I had to write it down. I was afraid it would escape my memory for good. I heard the sound of raindrops against my bedroom window. I rolled over, and reached for my eyeglasses, then quickly put them on. It was raining outside. I loved nothing more than to sleep during a storm. For me, it was cleansing and a sign that springtime was finally here. I knew it was there against my window, but the window was dry. I could still hear the constant "pitter-patter" but noticed the sounds were coming from inside the room. I felt a drop hit my forehead, then another one on my cheek. I quickly turned to my nightstand and reached out to switch on the lamp. In seconds, I watched droplets of water rain down upon the furniture—the table, the nightstand, the chair. I returned to conceal myself under the covers and continued to listen to the "pattering" of drops. It began to rain down harder. It was showering on my comforter, and drops hit my forehead and my eyeglasses.

Oh my God! A pipe must have burst upstairs in another room!

I wanted to move, but had no control. I wanted to run to the nurse's station and ask them to check upstairs. Again, I could not move. The dream had a mind of its own, and I had to wait it out. I had to wait to experience its plan. I slowly turned to look up at the ceiling, and became terrified and mesmerize at what hung above me. Inconceivably, water was pooling on the ceiling. How could this be? Water was defying gravity and quickly filling downward from the ceiling. Then I began to smell it. It was the unmistakable scent of seawater. The water was dark and cold and it began to churn and reach.

What is going on?

Suddenly, the room began to rock slowly from one side to another. I held on to the blanket. I could not make it stop. I closed my eyes tightly, but the rocking became more violent, and widening. The room was going to flip! The water from the ceiling began to crash against the walls. The pitch was terrifying, yet in the dream, I wanted it to take me. The feeling of seasickness built rapidly within my stomach.

Let go James. Just let go.

It was her voice. It was Jade! I opened my eyes and my body fell upward into the ceiling...into the waves...into her voice.

Come with me James.

For a few seconds my mind and body were disoriented. Up was down, down was up, and I could not discriminate between either. I struggled within the dark, beneath the rough and battering water. I held my breath for as long as I could. I was so happy to hear her voice, but I hated the blackness, and feared drowning. Suddenly, a flash of light struck my eyes. Then I felt it capture my body. Just as quickly as it came, the piercing ray of light disappeared. The glass bubble consumed my body, and I was finally able to breathe. Without hesitation, the transparent orb began to build speed. A startling thought filled my mind. I wondered why I did not suffer the physical effects one would expect to experience if travelling at this rate of speed. It was breathtaking and riveting. It was a rollercoaster ride unlike any known to man. I sat with my legs crossed and placed my hands comfortably at each side. We were going deeper. The vehicle dove rapidly as I sat unharmed in its grasp. Ridged and fractured seawalls began to fill my view. The grandeur of what I began to witness was beyond anything I could have imagined. The entire scope was larger than life, and from my small irrelevant perspective, I truly felt like a grain of sand by comparison. I looked up and saw the fish and dolphins. They remained up above me, swimming at a safe depth. The machine took me deeper until everything above me faded to a deep velvety black. I began to hear the resounding cries of whales. The sound penetrated through the bubble and into my chest. Within my heart, I became filled with warmth. I felt the connection I waited so long to feel. It was an unquestionable presence of love and oneness. Through tear-filled eyes, I began to see it. It was coming closer, and the orb was moving toward it as such an incredible speed. It had to be so far from the surface. Before my eyes, I began to see a massive structure of some kind.

"James…James!" Her annoying voice broke through.

The glass bubble dissolved and my body jolted upon the bed. I opened my eyes.

"It's time for your medication." It was Nurse Clemins, and she was yelling.

I looked up at her and hoped that someone would drop a house on her!

April 11, 2009
Saturday 11:04PM

I have been working hard with Tonya on my physical rehabilitation. I continued to push myself as far as possible. I no longer wanted to look ill. My mind was made up and I was going to do everything in my power to become more physically fit. Ian would come and keep me company in the gym, and of course, he would make sure I did not overdo it. Tonight Ian was with me while I worked on the leg press machine. I looked across the gym and our eyes locked. Sarah was there. She was walking quickly on the treadmill. I wanted to get up and introduce her to Ian. I stopped for a moment and turned toward Ian. It was time he met her! I was about to get up and grab a towel when I saw Sarah walk through the automatic door.

"Is everything okay, James?" Ian questioned. He didn't realize why I became distracted.

"I'm good…I'm good." I replied.

What was going on with Sarah? It bothered me when she would act like this. There was no reason to be so mysterious. I wanted her to finally meet Ian and see that he is genuine and trustworthy.

"I'm done for today Ian. Can we just hangout upstairs?"

Ian walked with me through the automatic door and toward the elevator. Sarah eluded me again today, and her behavior was getting on my nerves. I know that something is brewing…something I'm not ready for.

April 14, 2009
Tuesday 9:56PM

I woke from a deep sleep about twenty minutes ago. I was fast asleep with one arm resting outside the covers. It hung over the bed. I heard her voice and the undertone of a whale's cry.

I felt a gentle breeze come upon my head like a caressing hand. I felt my hair slowly move, as I rested on my back. The rush of sounds and the touch of the sea breeze were settling. I felt myself adrift on a boat. This boat was more like a wooden raft, and it did not have a sail. Then it touched me. She touched me. My entire arm was doused in water and I felt the bed teeter. My eyes opened quickly, and I sat up. The bedroom was quiet and my arm was dry, but I saw her leave the room. It was Sarah!

James, you must not let her control you...

The television was off but the moon shed enough light inside to make me feel safe. What is the meaning of this? Why is she doing this! I need answers. I want answers.

Jade! What is going on?

You know what to do...

I slipped out from the bed and walked into the bathroom. I switched the light on and began to wash my face. The mirror shot me a worn image.

FLASH

The bathroom door slammed shut and the light was extinguished. I stood there in the darkness. I fumbled to find the light switch, found it, but nothing happened each time I tried to flip the switch. My bare feet felt the water first, and it began to rise up my lower legs. I tried to open the door but it was locked. The water was now at my bellybutton, and continually rising. I pushed hard and used the force of my body to open the door. On the third try, the door flung open and I fell to the floor. There was no water. Everything was bone dry.

You must not give in to her!

April 16, 2009
Thursday 10:41PM

For the past week, I did everything I was asked to do. I did not complain about anything, to anyone. I was polite and civil toward the entire staff. I spent most of my time here in my room. I would meet Tonya at her office, and then spend time in the lap pool. Ian arranged his work schedule to be with me for supper, and accompanied me to and from the cafeteria. Tonight we finished eating then watched an hour of TV. He was tired. By eight-thirty, he decided to leave. I walked him to the door and watched him until he entered the elevator. He waved at me then disappeared. I heard the elevator door close and reentered my room.

"James." She whispered my name, and I stood frozen in the moment. Then she called once again. Her voice was raspy and haunting. I could not shake the eerie sensation. It came upon me anytime I heard her voice. I stood with my back to her room, and heard her door slowly creak open. In the process, I turned around. It was Sarah. She did not enter the hallway; instead, she produced only her head. Her eyes were empty, and under them were dark, eggplant colored circles. She looked very pale and in the moment, she resembled an evil porcelain doll.

Jerk...Jerk...Tick

"What do you want? Why are you bothering me?" I inquired. My stomach turned.

"What I have to say to you is inside one of your books!" Sarah's voice was animated and anomalous.

She did not give me a chance to respond. Sarah quickly pulled her head back inside her room and slammed her door. I heard what she said, but it took a few moments to register. I hurriedly entered my room and closed the door. She had been in my room, again! When? Why?

Inside one of your books!

I crept inside and scanned the room. I had placed two books on the nightstand, and had another handful in a plastic bag beside it. I went over, picked up the first one, and thumbed through it. I did it again, and again. I tried to find a note...a letter...something. I put it down and began inspecting the second book. Was she playing a game with me? I began to feel the room close in on me.

You might have to look through all the books.

Just before I put it down, there it was. Sarah did not leave a conventional note; however, she circled words and letters within the book. I turned back to the beginning then quickly paged through it until I saw the first circle. I sat on the bed and began to unravel her sick code. What was she up to? Page by page I turned and noted each letter or word in order.

She was in your room and you didn't even know it.

As I continued to decipher her message, I realized how troubled she was. This was an eerie and inappropriate way to get my attention. I began to feel sorry for her. She was definitely mentally ill, and something beyond a brain disease, was at play. Her irrational behavior was proof enough for me. I attentively wrote down everything she circled until there were no more markings. It did not hit me until I began to piece the letters and words together. I sat there on the bed and began to read her mysterious message.

you believe Ian / he is lying to you / I am angry / they are medically abusing us / we will never leave this place / we are lab rats / you have betrayed all of us / he will never take you back home / you will die in this place / Ian knows the truth / he signed you over to them / i am angry / I thought you believed me / i will see you soon / I am going to kill all of them

I felt a haunting chill as I read back her message. I did not know what to do. Our doors did not have locks, and she could enter my room at her own leisure. What did I do to make her so mad? Do I show this to Doctor O'Shea...to Ian...to anyone?

Oh My God! The meds are beginning to work. Don't sleep tonight. Don't sleep tonight. Don't sleep tonight.

I tore the page out of the white pad, folded it, and hid it underneath my mattress. It became more difficult to keep my eyes open. I decided to leave the room light on and got under the covers. I propped myself up as much as I could and listened to the silence.

Stay awake!

I heard my thoughts and Jade's voice ring through my ears. All I wanted was to hear nothing!

James? James? Can you hear me? I am here!

April 20, 2009
Monday 9:10 PM

I woke up this morning, but not in my own room. This room was entirely painted in white. Even the door with its tiny window, was an eggshell white. The room was extremely small with only a light switch on the wall, a single bed, and a wooden chair. There were no windows, and nothing hanging on the walls. It was bare—sanitarily and clinically empty.

Why am I here? What happened?

I couldn't move my body without feeling fatigue. I felt groggy and disconnected. I rested there for at least thirty minutes before I noticed someone looking in from the small window on the door. Seconds later, I heard the door unlock and Doctor O'Shea entered.

"Good afternoon James, how are you feeling?" Her voice was soft and calm.

"Where am I? Where's Ian? Why am I here?" I had to reconnect.

Doctor O'Shea walked over to the wooden chair and sat down. This was the first time I saw her without a briefcase, folder, writing pad, or a tape recorder.

"You are right outside my office, and Ian is down the hall." She responded.

"Why am I here?" I asked.

Doctor O'Shea waited for a moment before answering my question. "Do you remember what happened in your room four nights ago?" Her voice was unsteady.

I looked at her. "Four nights ago?" My mind was racing and I could not focus.

"You are here for your own protection. We have been monitoring you." Doctor O'Shea was delicate with her words.

For my protection? Monitoring?

Unexpectedly, an ice-cold awareness came over me. First, there was a single flash, then another, then another.

FLASH

The room suddenly began to grow larger, and larger. The ceiling and walls began to change. A dark pair of hands began to stretch and pull the room out of shape. Various colors and furniture began to fill the spaces around me. I was back inside my hospital room, in bed, and under my comforter. Without pause, the room became darker, and right away, fear grabbed a hold of me. There was a sudden moan, then a cackle. It was terrifying. I heard her voice, and it was raspy and sharp. She was crawling on the floor toward my bed. I peered over the comforter and saw Sarah. She continued to creep along the floor until she got to the foot of my bed.

I will kill Ian!

"James!" I heard Doctor O'Shea's voice in the distance. "James!"

You betrayed all of us!

I tried to lay as still as possible. Fear continued to swim through my body. I remember looking over at the clock. The crimson numbers of the digital display had shown 3AM. I had fallen asleep! My heart rate increased, and it was difficult to take a breath. She placed her hands on the foot of my bed, but did not show her face. Although pale moonlight entered through my window, it failed to expose what Sarah was doing.

Turn on the lights and grab your glasses. Hurry!

Suddenly, Sarah came at me. She jumped onto the bed and crawled up onto my chest. I tried to move but she was too fast. The pillow was ripped from under my head and pressed down upon my face. I searched for the energy to fight back, and was able to grab the pillow to take a breath. I screamed as loud as I could. I reached out to find the lamp on the nightstand. Before I could use it to defend myself, Sarah took it from my hand and threw it into the air. Within the darkness, I heard the lamp make contact. My rack of CD's crashed to the floor. I continued to yell and struggle with Sarah, but I knew my time was running out.

"You betrayed all of us!" Sarah yelled. "You are so weak!"

Oh my God! She is going to kill me!

I fought for control of the pillow, and in the distance, I heard the sound of running feet enter the corridor outside the room. I continued to yell and my hands found her hair. I hoped she would give up, so I pulled as hard as I could.

"I will kill Ian next!" Sarah shouted. "I will get that son-of-a-bitch!"

The pounding footsteps were getting closer; however, Sarah had more strength in her than I did at that moment. The medications and Sarah were victorious. She forced the pillow over my face and I remember fading away into silence.

"James!"

In the distance, I continued to hear Doctor O'Shea call for me. I felt caught between two spaces in time. The doctor was at one side of a tunnel, and I remained helpless at the other. The only thing I could do was wait for Sarah to kill me. My body wanted to move. I wanted to escape, but no matter what I did, I was frozen and overtaken. Breathe! Keep breathing! I felt the pressure of Sarah's hand through the pillow, and heard the muffling of her voice.

Why didn't you help us? Now you'll pay!

"James! It's me...James!" I heard his voice, and then felt his hands. The room was bathed in light. The transformation was so rapid. Everything began to dissolve and the room became brighter and smaller. The darkened hands were burned by the light, and I opened my eyes. Sarah was gone. Then I saw him. Ian was looking down at me, his hands holding my face.

"I'm here, I'm here! It's Ian."

I was back in the white room and Ian was with me. Sarah was gone.

Jerk...Tick...Tick

My lungs searched for air. "She tried to kill me! She said she was going to kill you too! It was Sarah!" I had to let him know. I had to warn him.

"It's okay. You are okay." Ian wiped the sweat from my brow. He turned toward Doctor O'Shea and began to yell. "No more! Do you hear me? No more! I hold you personally responsible for this! Where was your staff? Where the hell was your security?"

Doctor O'Shea got up from the chair and walked out.

"I'm taking you back to your room. I'm going to stay with you for a while."

I felt safe and I knew Ian was going to hold a 'come-to-Jesus-meeting' with every single person on the payroll of CNS! He was going to make sure Doctor O'Shea moved Sarah far away from me. The magnitude of the situation suddenly hit me, and now I feared the safety of the others. Would Sarah try to attack Liz, Mickey, or Walter? I have to warn them!

"I'm going to get Frank. I'll be right back." Ian got up from the edge of the twin bed and left the room.

I shut my eyes and thought of the beach…the sun…the water…my seal…I did not hear her voice this time. I waited for the bubble to snatch me from this room, but it never came.

Jade where are you?

The small holding room was peaceful and safe, and I hoped that I would never see Sarah again.

May 1, 2009
Friday 11:46 PM

Ian stayed with me the days following the incident with Sarah. I hadn't seen her once since, nor did I hear a single sound from her room. Even though it made me happy that she was gone, the silence was quite odd. Anytime I asked the Staff about her, they simply changed the subject. I finally asked Ian if he knew where she was. I could tell that the subject made him uncomfortable, but he told me that Doctor O'Shea had her transferred to another facility. It was great to have Ian here more often. He knew I missed our cats, and he filled me in on their feline antics. It was just like the good old days.

Tonight was the night, and I opened up to him completely. I told him about Jade, the seal, my dreams of the ocean, the glass machine, and everything else. He didn't think I was going crazy; instead, he let me talk. He listened as I recalled my experiences. Ian always listened to me, always. Was he going to tell Doctor O'Shea? I had faith that he would keep everything between us.

Later on, Ian asked me about my session today, so I filled him in. I told him that I was surprised that Doctor O'Shea actually thought about my idea. She took my advice about holding a group session. I walked into the office, and to my surprise, Mickey, Walter, and Liz were there. Everyone sat in a semi-circle in front of the Doctor's desk. As soon as

I entered the room, I went straight to Liz. She was still very upset and a box of tissues sat on her lap. She was happy to see me and she knew as soon as I hugged her, that the feeling was mutual. I looked at Mickey and Walter and did my best to let them know how great it was to see them too. Mickey was a bit more receptive than Walter was, but I didn't take it personally.

"Good morning James." Doctor O'Shea interrupted.

I turned around and acknowledged her, then sat down at the chair beside Liz. I wondered if the doctor told the group about the small video camera propped up on the filing cabinet. I noticed it as soon as I walked in. I did not mention it to the others, and it only confirmed what I had already knew—Doctor O'Shea had to be in control of everything.

"I think this is great!" I exclaimed, looking at the group.

Doctor O'Shea began taping the session. "Today is Friday, May 1st 2009. I am conducting a group session today with four patients." She placed the tape recorder down on the desk and took out her white pad. "Who would like to go first?"

"I just want to know where you moved Cathy." Liz began to sob.

I knew Liz needed a release, and I was relieved that she started the session with Cathy's sudden disappearance. I was hoping Doctor O'Shea would be a bit softer with Liz.

"Jesus Christ!" Walter hollered. "I could be watching the news right now. Isn't it enough that we meet separately once a week?"

"Walter!" I pleaded. "Can't you see that Liz is falling apart over Cathy, and the fact that we just lost Kitty." I turned to look at Doctor O'Shea. She looked at me and widened her eyes.

"Well, I know she's upset!" Walter barked. "But what can we do? We're old, sonny. People our age die!"

"Why do you have to be such an ass, Walter?" Mickey reprimanded. "If you're gonna be an idiot, then go watch your damned Fox News!"

Liz began to cry harder. "You are such an insensitive pig!"

"Okay, let's regroup." Doctor O'Shea requested. "Please calm down or I will have to end the session."

Tick…Jerk

Walter took in several heavy breaths from his oxygen tank. The sound was quite disturbing, the type I could never get used to hearing. I could see Walter was upset and this group session may not have been such a great idea. Mickey, on the other hand, was less erratic and more levelheaded, and did not seem to mind the meeting.

"Walter, are you okay?" I was truly concerned. "Don't get yourself so worked up."

"I'm fine." He squawked, then turned and peered at Doctor O'Shea. "Let's just get on with this."

Walter settled down and Doctor O'Shea relaxed back into her chair.

Tick…Jerk…Jerk

"Liz," Doctor O'Shea started. "Please share your feelings with the group."

Liz dried her eyes and cleared her throat. "Well, you know why I am upset." She did her best to maintain her composure. "I know you won't tell me where Cathy is, but can you please let us know how she's doing?"

"I don't want you to worry, everything is fine." Doctor O'Shea announced.

"Thank you Doctor, this is just so overwhelming, and I miss her." Liz was relieved. "I'm not even sure if Cathy knows that Kitty passed."

"Who called for this group thing? And, why weren't we asked if we wanted to participate?" Walter growled, utterly railroading Liz's emotions.

I looked at Doctor O'Shea then back at the group. "It was me. I hoped that we could get to know each other." I felt that my plan was about to backfire.

Jerk…Jerk…Tick

"Sonny, I'm not an alcoholic, and this isn't an AA meeting!" Walter was a bitter old man. "Nobody asked you to round us up like cattle, and screw up our day!"

"I'm sorry Walter, I didn't mean to ruin anyone's day." I felt horrible. My intentions were good, and for Christ's sake, I did not want to be the one responsible for giving Walter a coronary!

"Can you give the kid a break?" Mickey turned and shouted at Walter.

"Honey, I think this was a great idea." Liz reassured me. "It is great to be around young people. It makes an old woman like me feel needed."

Doctor O'Shea was restless and moving uncomfortably in her chair. "Let's lower the volume and keep it civilized."

Tick...Jerk...Jerk

"Well, I just think this is useless." Walter bellowed. "And how come the young girl isn't here? Was she excused from this little get-together?"

I was wondering the same thing, although I was extremely content that Sarah was separated from the rest of us. The doctor didn't answer Walter's question regarding Sarah, and I felt even more relieved that her whereabouts weren't mentioned.

"Walter, what counts is that we are here. I didn't mean any harm. If you want to leave, you can."

I turned to Doctor O'Shea for backup, but she said nothing. She said not a damned thing!

"Isn't that right Doctor O'Shea?" I tried again, and looked at her with daggered eyes.

She crossed her arms and looked back at me. I wanted to make Walter aware that he was not going to be forced to take part in anything he did not want to. However, Ms. O'Shea was not going to help! She sat there on her royal throne and I knew what she was thinking—'You wanted this group session. Are you happy now?'

"Walter if you are going to continue to disrupt the session, you can leave." Liz gently suggested. She sensed the friction between the Doctor and me.

Walter didn't say a word. He huffed and mumbled as he maneuvered his wheelchair from the group, then to the door. Shortly after, Walter was gone.

"Honey, it's okay. We are glad to be here with you." Liz looked at me, and then looked at Mickey.

Tick...Tick

I had an idea. "Maybe we can get together a couple of nights a week? I enjoy checkers and card games. Maybe we could eat lunch as a group, a couple of days a week?"

Both Mickey and Liz were very receptive toward my idea, but the tension in the room did not lessen. Doctor O'Shea sat there and did not say a word.

"I will try to talk to Walter." I looked at Liz and Mickey. "I can give it another shot."

I knew Walter was going to be a difficult one to win over, however if he saw us together more often, he might just warm up to the idea. I wanted to understand why Walter was so angry and blatantly mean. There had to be a skeleton or two I could help rattle out of his closet.

"Doctor O'Shea?" I turned to ask her a question, but this time she was too busy writing notes. "Would it be possible for the group to visit the courtyard? The weather is changing and it would be great to get some fresh air." I waited for her response.

"Let's take it one day at a time, James." She put her writing pad down and folded her hands on her desk. "We need to continue to move forward with our one-on-one sessions and maybe soon that will be possible."

Tick...Tick...Jerk

I did not want to hear that same excuse from her again. This place seemed more like solitary confinement in a maximum-security prison, than a full-fledged medical facility. I requested fresh air, not a truckload of plutonium, or water from the moon!

She wants to keep you here! Sarah was right!

"What about Mickey, Walter, and Liz? Why are they not permitted to visit the courtyard for lunch or at least a change of scenery?" I didn't see anything wrong with this simple request, especially when they are entirely alone. No one ever visits them. Not only are they old, but their next breath might be their last.

"James, we talked about this before and there are reasons for why we have specific rules." Doctor O'Shea's response was patronizing but mostly irrational.

"Jesus, Mary, and Joseph!" I belted. "They are old for Christ's sake. It's not like they are going to break out of your precious hospital and hold up a goddammed bank!"

"Honey, don't worry about us." Liz jumped in. She tried to calm me down. "We are fine. We keep each other company."

"I am sorry Liz, but I disagree with Doctor O'Shea." I shot the Doctor a hateful look. I was not about to let her get away with such bull! "Frank said patients are allowed out in the courtyard as long as they are accompanied by a staff member." I waited for an explanation, and hoped she wouldn't hand me another line of crap!

"Yes, that is the policy James. However, I make the rules for my patients, and I stand firmly by my decision." Doctor O'Shea forced.

Tick...Tick...Tick

"What about your patients and their needs?" I inquired. "You get to leave this place every day, and go wherever you wish, while we are stuck here."

"Honey, don't get yourself worked up." Liz rubbed my shoulder. "Everything is fine."

"Liz, everything is not fine. It's not like we are asking for anything outrageous!" I exclaimed. "The last time I heard, getting out and breathing fresh air was actually beneficial to humans!"

Doctor O'Shea picked up the phone and called the nurse's station. I could see by the look on her face that she was finished. I had crossed the line, and I had pushed her over the edge. I embarrassed her in front of her patients. Most of all, I had the nerve to question the almighty Doctor!

Good! She's getting pissed off!

"Our group session is over." Doctor O'Shea spoke into the phone, and then hung it up. Seconds later, she looked at us. "I may entertain future meetings, but not anytime soon."

Tick...Jerk...Jerk

It was obvious that the session did not go as well as I hoped, but Doctor O'Shea definitely failed to help in any way. She looked quite pleased that it had flopped.

Frank and Nurse Collins entered the room moments later, and I noticed Frank's face was red as an apple. He failed to look at me once, even though I did everything but scream his name to try to make eye contact.

I began to stand up from my chair, but Doctor O'Shea asked me to stay. I watched and waited for Frank and Nurse Collins to assist Liz and Mickey out into the hallway.

"Frank, please close the door." Doctor O'Shea's voice was courteous but sharp.

Oh, Lord! She's really going to ream me!

The door closed and she remained seated at her desk. She looked at me for quite some time before she addressed me.

Tick…Tick…Jerk

"So how did that go?" Her voice was low and surprisingly calm. She pushed herself closer to the desk.

"I really didn't mean to make waves. I guess I will never understand why you choose to keep us confined in here." I tried to battle the topic once more. This time I lowered my tone and tried to be civil.

"I am no longer going to debate this with you." She remained calm, but her overbearing need to control the world—my world, was not easy for me to digest. "This topic is closed and we will not revisit it again."

"I truly get it Doc." I retorted. "Anything outside your box of rules is out of the question."

In no way was I trying to be belligerent, nor was I trying to strike another argument. All I wanted was to comprehend her motives. Simply, I wanted to understand her rationale. Doctor O'Shea sat back in her chair and crossed her arms. Not once did it ever occur to her that her own behavior was part of the problem. She is a Psychiatrist! Why couldn't she recognize that her empty explanations and pathetic rules caused most of our "one-on-one's" to be overtly counterproductive?

"I can see that you are upset James." She began. "I think you should go back to your room and take time to reflect on today's session."

I was at a loss for words. She shut me down instantly with yet again, another wave of her magic "patronizing" wand. I stood up, looked at her, and then turned to open the office door. I said nothing; however, I let the slamming sound of the door behind me express precisely how I felt!

May 9, 2009
Saturday 11:28PM

I waited until after dinner. Once we returned to my room from the cafeteria, I laid it out for Ian. I told him that I could no longer deal with Doctor O'Shea's nasty attitude and the way she belittles me. He said that he didn't want me to stress, nor did he want to see me upset. It was very simple. I told him that he needed to do something to put her in check, or I would. I told him that I would not attend our Friday sessions and I would avoid her like the plague. Ian already had a discussion with Doctor O'Shea after the incident with Sarah, but whatever he said obviously did not work. I pushed harder, and made sure Ian knew I was serious. I told him that I would also refuse to take any medication, unless something was done. He understood how trapped I felt, and angry. The fact remained—I had not had a breath of fresh air in over a year. He did not want me to miss my meetings, or stop taking my meds, so he said he would speak with her.

I felt more relaxed now that Ian was staying here with me. It wasn't every day, but at least three or four days a week. Tonight was one of the nights Ian returned home to his apartment. He wanted to make sure the cats were okay, and needed to do his laundry. I missed my babies and hated Doctor O'Shea even more for not allowing me to see them. What did she have to gain from being so bitter? Doesn't she see how much pain I am in? It would make such a difference if I saw Dusk and Caesar. Why did she choose to remove them from my life? All I have is a picture of them.

I hoped that I would never forget them. My cats were all I had left.

May 10, 2009
Sunday 10:57PM

About an hour ago, I heard a knock on my door. To my surprise, it was Mickey. I was happy to see him, and asked him to come inside. He declined, and stated that he just wanted to stop by to thank me for the other day. He put his hand out toward me, and I extended mine. We shook.

"It's okay Ace! It's great that you thought of bringing us together. A friend in need is a friend indeed."

FLASH

This time the light was so strong against my eyes, and it felt like being hit in the face with a laser beam. I opened my eyes to find myself inside of a workshop. Tools of all kind hung on walls, some rested on workbenches. "Come here Ace." Mickey's voice filled the space and I saw a teen boy walk over to where Mickey was working. Mickey was younger, and he showed the boy shelving units and furniture he had just finished building. The young boy looked familiar. I looked at both of them, and they had a special bond. I noticed it right away, and I felt it deep inside. The picture was perfect and so was the incredible love they shared.

"You can do anything you want. You can be anything you want.

Don't forget that!" Mickey spoke to the young boy, and the boy smiled back at him.

Suddenly, Mickey and the boy turned toward me. I saw the child— it was a younger me. The visions flooded through, and I saw the boy and Mickey building things, creating things, drawing things—the filmstrip of memories invaded my eyes. The boy loved him, and looked up to him. Their bond was so strong—unbreakable. The boy transformed into a teen, and Mickey grew older. They remained close and their connection was untarnished. The wave of memories continued, and I saw them sitting talking, and laughing.

FLASH

I saw the vision—it was Christmas. The scream was heartbreaking—it came from a woman. I saw the Christmas tree and it became blurry in my watery eyes. I felt the gaping hole within my chest—once it was my heart. I felt the loss. The image was a snapshot of the teen—it was me. I was shattered. I walked through the house and entered the basement. The basement was where he used to find Mickey—where I could find Mickey. However, the basement was no longer alive with the sounds of ban-saws, nail hammering, or childish laughter between them. It was quiet. The basement was filled with death-stolen silence. The vision was through the eyes of young adult— a seventeen-year-old boy. Mickey was forever gone, and so was a part of that boy—me.

FLASH

I heard Mickey's voice as I entered through the light. "I am fine. You can let go. I am sorry for leaving you."

I was back at my room, standing with the door wide open, and tears in my eyes. Mickey was no longer standing there. What just happened? Where did he go? I closed my bedroom door and sat at my window.

Journal, journal, in my hands, who's the craziest across this land?

May 13, 2009
Wednesday 10:11PM

Today was another tough day. I was about to begin another session in the lap pool. Tonya adjusted the flow, and I continued with a low impact workout. I loved to swim and missed it so much. Tonya stood by to monitor me, and usually that would have bothered me, but not today. I quickly noticed that I was tired and worn, and within three minutes, I gave into the flow and rested alongside the unit. Tonya was supportive. She was truly a genuine, loving, and caring person. In her line of work, it was a requirement. She saw how defeated I looked and came over to where I was resting. She placed her hand on my head.

"You need to be proud of yourself. You continue to amaze me each day, now I only wish you saw that in yourself." Her voice was kind and completely authentic.

I did not reply, but she recognized my pain through the tears falling from my eyes. That was the defining moment for me. I made a silent pact with myself.

You will get stronger! You must get stronger! Never give up!

I exited the pool and told Tonya that I wanted to relax in the hot tub. It was actually an oversized stainless steel bathtub with a variety of jets. Tonya told me that she'd give me twenty minutes to myself. The water was comfortably hot. It made my entire body relax and eased the soreness of my weakened muscles. I rested the back of my head on the rim of the tub, and looked up at the ceiling. I hated feeling this feeble. Some days I felt strong, then the next, so weak. I hated feeling trapped and unable to go home. Although I never wanted to see her again, I finally understood what made Sarah unstable and disparaged, and what put her over the edge—This place! CNS!

You can't let that happen to you! You have to be stronger!

Don't give in! You must not give in!

I tried to focus. I wanted to clear my mind of all thoughts. I felt the pulsing water massage my arms and legs, and focused on the sound of the invigorating jets. I cupped my hands and bathed my face with the warm, soothing water. There were no thoughts. I found a single moment of serenity. The moments were rare, very rare indeed. I missed my parents so much. They are everything to me. Their love always got me through the most difficult times. Summer was coming and so was my birthday. Mom and I were one day apart, and we always celebrated ours together. It was so special to me. I always wondered if she knew just how special it meant to me. She loved me so deeply, and I wish I could have one of her fantastic hugs. Then I thought of my father. I looked up to him in so many ways. Figuratively speaking, he is the kind of person who would give you the shirt off his back if you needed it! Many times, he did just that for me. He came through for me when all hope seemed to vanish, and when life began to twist itself into a massive tornado. I never truly told him all of this, but I hope he knows. My parent's love for one another always amazed me. I used to watch them together. They loved one another unconditionally. I was lucky to be there when they celebrated their fiftieth wedding anniversary. They allowed us, their children, the honor of renewing their vows and giving each of them away to the other. It was a great day. It was an amazing day. It was a day filled with love and happy tears. There was no other day like it!

Then there are my siblings—my fabulous brothers and sisters. What a dysfunctional bunch they are…but MY dysfunctional bunch! I miss each of them! I miss the laughter, the noise, and the Italian bravados. Mostly, I miss the way they looked at me. I miss the way they loved me. I am the seventh of eight children, but earned the honor of being the 'go-to' whenever they needed advice, a shoulder to lean on, or simply an ear to listen. I would do anything to hear their voices.

The moment of reflection did not last long. I felt the bottom of the stainless steel tub disappear, and down I plummeted into a dark abyss of water. I was being pulled downward by evil stronghold. I looked upward to see the outline of the tub, and the patch of light from within it.

You belong down here with me! You could have saved us! Now you will never leave!

It was Sarah! I heard her voice just below me in the void, and feared that she would pull me down, deeper, deeper into the blackness. I impulsively fought the descending pull of the water. I had very little breath left, but I continued to struggle upward against the surge of water. The rim of the tub, and the light, were getting closer. I saw her face. It was Tonya. She was looking down at me. Her words were incoherent, but I could tell she was yelling and shouting down at me. The light was getting brighter and brighter, and I knew I had to get to the surface soon.

"James! It's me…Tonya…James!" I heard her voice. This time it was clear and comprehendible.

I opened my eyes and felt the bottom of the hydrotherapy tub beneath me.

"James, I heard you yelling…You had fallen asleep…I rushed in here and you were splashing around." Tonya was beside herself with concern. "Are you okay? Do you need me to call Dr. O'Shea? Frank? Ian?"

"No…no…don't worry…I was just dreaming." My heart was pounding. "I'm okay."

I couldn't let her see how disturbed I was. I let Tonya help me out of the tub, and onto my feet. The entire surface of the floor, beneath, and around the tub was covered with water.

She carefully assisted me, and we carefully maneuvered ourselves toward the exit. I slipped my feet into a pair of flip-flops and quickly put on my bathrobe.

"I'm going to go back to my room, Tonya." I looked at her. "Thanks for everything."

Tonya was still shaken. "You take care of yourself, James. We'll continue with the lap pool, unless you feel otherwise."

"No, that sounds great, and I'd appreciate if what happened here stays here." I hoped she would go along.

"It is fine, James. We all have bad dreams." Tonya opened the door. I headed back to my room, and Tonya headed back into her office.

James, you cannot let her win... You must prepare...

May 15, 2009
Friday 11:51 PM

Today's session with Dr. O'Shea went exactly as I expected. I had played nice with the entire staff and made sure everyone witnessed the leaf I had turned over. I smiled more. I said thank you and hello incessantly. I killed each of them with kindness. Doctor O'Shea began the session as usual. She began taping the meeting and read the weekly reports aloud.

"Nurse Clemins only had one grievance." Doctor O'Shea read Nurse Clemins' comment to herself, and then looked up at me. "What was that all about?"

I giggled. "Well, she came to administer my meds and she looked tired and unraveled. I told her that her perm looked like a bird's nest, and suggested that she take some time for herself." I explained myself to Doctor O'Shea, but the Ice Princess did not find any humor in it at all. I, on the other hand, thought it was hyena worthy!

Doctor O'Shea looked at me and was speechless. I wanted to lighten the moment, especially when she had already assumed that I had done something so unforgivable to one of her Staff!

"I didn't mean anything by it." I tried not to laugh. "She looked so worn-out and I only meant to say that she should take a break. Either that, or change her hair-dresser."

"Okay, let's move on." Doctor O'Shea rustled through the nurse's notes. "I see that the Staff as a whole has seen a big change in you."

"Well, I've been exercising more often, and swimming in the lap pool. I am getting stronger." I had to set my plan into motion with the Doctor. "Most of all, I had to realize that I can't expect to go home without giving it my all!"

"I am glad to hear that James. It is important that you stay on this track." Doctor O'Shea was convincing. "Everyone here wants to help you. All of us intend to be a part of your rehabilitation."

She wasn't being sincere. Doctor O'Shea was smarter than that. She was playing a game of her own. Nevertheless, I chose to go along with it.

"How are you sleeping?" She investigated.

"I believe I am finally getting used to the medications. I have no trouble sleeping at night." Again, I didn't want her to know the truth. The poisons she prescribed were often screwing with me.

Tick...Jerk...Jerk

"Good. It is important that you get enough rest, especially now that Tonya has expanded your PT." Doctor O'Shea continued to play nice, and I reciprocated.

"As you know, Ian has rearranged his schedule and is with me more often. I know I still have to rely on others to get to where I need to be." I began to tell her more of what she wanted to hear. "It's not easy to admit that I need help, but I know I can't do it all by myself."

The doctor began to write on her pad. I looked at the tape recorder and continued to speak.

"It's been so hard. I don't want the Staff to dislike me. I want them to respect me and of course I want to respect them."

Doctor O'Shea never lifted her head; however, I did not want her to interrupt my magnificent performance.

"I appreciate that you have kept Sarah away." Doctor O'Shea continued to listen. "I want you to know that I don't blame you for what happened. Who would have known that Sarah was going to attack me?"

Doctor O'Shea looked surprised. "What matters now James is that we move forward." She spoke softly and with a smile. "Anytime you feel nervous or intimidated, please notify anyone on duty. I have instructed the staff to contact me night or day."

"Thank you so much." I laid it on as thick as maple syrup. "I really like being able to talk to you like this. It is so important that I am able to trust you."

"That's what I am here for." She replied. "I am glad that we have made a breakthrough."

She had no clue. I knew that Ian ripped into her last night! He truly made a dent in her designer frame. I couldn't stand the sight of her, let alone the sound of her condescending voice! The remainder of the session was like playing a game of catch. We both played nicely and didn't throw the ball too hard.

Nevertheless, we were playing a game.

June 11, 2009
Thursday 9:44PM

James, you are almost ready. I will come for you soon.
I woke to hear the sound of her voice. It was soft and warm, just as always.

"James, it's time to get up. It is almost 9AM." Another woman's voice punctured the silence, but it was not Jade's.

I opened my eyes and saw it was Nurse Clemins. "You slept in today. It's time to get up and take your medication. You're late."

I sat up and rested my back against the headboard. "Must you be so friggin rude?"

Nurse Clemins didn't respond. She came over and handed me the cup of meds. I followed the normal ritual, and waited for her to leave.

"Doctor O'Shea is going to meet you here in your room in an hour." Ms. Clemins notified me, and then left as abruptly as she entered.

Today was Thursday, not Friday. And, why was she coming to my room? It didn't matter because I had no say.

10AM
I had finished showering and got dressed and ready for Doctor O'Shea. I was a bit startled when Ian walked in the room.

"Hi." Ian began. "Doctor O'Shea called me this morning and asked if I could meet her in your room." Ian was a little out of breath. "Is everything okay?"

"Your guess is as good as mine." I replied. "I just go along with whatever. It's not like I have a say in anything she decides."

Ian looked at me and I know he understood what I was feeling. His facial expression was filled with hopelessness, and it screamed—'I'm doing the best I can!'

***

"Good morning," Doctor O'Shea began, as she walked into my bedroom. "I am sorry for the inconvenience, but I am having some work done in my office."

"Today is Thursday." I replied. I couldn't wait to hear her excuse.

Ian looked at me with the 'please do not start anything' look. He quickly moved over to the small table and pulled out a chair for her.

"Yes, I am aware of that, James." The Doctor sat down, and placed her briefcase at her side. "I will not be available tomorrow." There was a short pause, and then she took hold of the conversation. "Doctor Swartz and I have been examining James' progress, and we feel that it is in his best interest to move to the next step." She looked at Ian the entire time, and acted as if I was absent from the room.

"I am here." I resounded. "Do I have a say in anything that has to do with me?"

"I apologize, James." Doctor O'Shea's voice was as usual, patronizing. "Of course your opinion is important."

Ian cut in. "So, let's cut to the chase." He finally witnessed the way she spoke to me, and it annoyed him. "What is the next step?"

Doctor O'Shea opened her briefcase and pulled out a white folder, and handed it to Ian. I saw the cover. There was a picture of a wide building with open grounds. It resembled a university, and within the photo, I saw Joshua trees and tall cactuses.

"We will be moving James to another institution." She informed us. "We are affiliated with this facility, and they believe James is a perfect candidate for their new program." She paused, and then dropped the bomb. "The facility is in Arizona."

I sat there—stunned. Ian had the folder in his hands and looked through its contents as she spoke. "When?" Ian asked.

I knew it from that moment. Ian was not going to put up a fight to keep me on the east coast. It was true—Ian did not have control. CNS did.

"July 1st." Doctor O'Shea replied, and then got up from the chair. "I have a meeting, so I must go." She looked down at Ian. "I will call you in a few days." Then she turned toward me. "I will see you next Friday for our session."

Doctor O'Shea left the room. She acted as if nothing just happened. Moreover, she left both of us in shock—in silence.

Ian looked at me, and then stood up. "I'll be right back." He was in distress and was about to crack. "We will be fine. I will make sure of it."

Most of the day Ian was gone, and he said he was doing everything he could to make this right. My appetite was gone, and I sat at my window until the sun went down. I wanted to tell him that I was okay. I knew everything was going to work out. I wanted him to know that I was at peace with what was coming.

June 17, 2009
Wednesday 10:37 PM

Doctor O'Shea's opinions or points of view no longer mattered. I remained on task and put all of my energy into preparing for my trip. Frank watched me like a hawk, and I wished I could tell him everything. I let him hang around and even assist me on the occasions when Tonya was with other patients. He never questioned my actions. Frank remained helpful and by my side as often as he could. I decided to spend every possible hour working on my body. I swam in the lap pool more often and began to build strength and endurance. I worked closely with Tonya. I continued to utilize the weight room daily and remained focused and confident. I began weeks ago, and now I was able to complete upwards of ten miles a day on the stationary bike. Tonya worked extra hard with me and I tried to tapper my anger, and my fears, but more importantly, I began to find my center. I stopped thinking of Sarah, and noticed that she didn't have an effect on me anymore. I had to stop thinking about her, and I had to worry about myself. The ticking and jerking happened through the day, but not as frequently. The dreams continued, and Jade continued to show me so much more. It didn't matter where I was or what I was doing. The flashes would come at any time. While in the gym, the cafeteria, or simply, in the shower, the flashes would arrive without warning. I spoke of these experiences more often with Ian, and as he did in the past, he listened. I told him that these flashes would happen randomly. He asked me if they ever happened while he was present. I was honest and said yes. I recounted a time this week when he and I were eating lunch in the cafeteria. I recalled the conversation. Ian was discussing his work, and had stated that he was going to have to fire an employee. That is when the sudden flash of light entered my eyes. Sound disappeared into a vacuum, and I felt my body being pulled inward, as if my soul was de-shelled, separated from my skin. He asked me how it physically felt when it happened, and I told him that there was no pain or discomfort. I told Ian that the feeling was strange and almost divine and oddly familiar—déjà vu-like.

Ian sat speechless, but attentive. I explained to him that once the flashes resigned, all time remained intact. Although the transmissions lasted seconds, it seemed I had been gone forever.

I asked Ian if he thought I was going crazy, and he replied in the fashion only Ian could.

"If you're going crazy, then I don't want to be sane!"

June 19, 2009
Friday 11:09 PM

I worked out most of the day following my session with Doctor O'Shea. She tried her best to rustle my feathers today. She picked and prodded, and did everything she could to find out what I had been up to.

"I must say, your entire attitude and demeanor has changed." She began. "For the best of course."

It no longer bothered me, her tricks of the trade, nor the old-fashioned reverse psychology. I wanted so badly to tell her. I wanted to throw it out there, like a worm-bated hook. I knew better, though. She still had the upper hand and full control over my life, here at CNS. I was not about to compromise myself to a verbal scrimmage with her, nor was I about to take ten steps backwards. I had worked too diligently to give in to her game.

"Tonya reports that you are spending additional time in the pool and gym." She made that statement, but I knew she wanted to know the reason why.

"Yes." I started. "I realized that exercising was helping with the effects of the medications."

"Absolutely." She agreed. "I am pleased with your initiatives."

Doctor O'Shea went on about how pleased she was to see that I was making such headway. She pointed out that exercising would continue to help me deal with emotional issues and possibly lessen negative behaviors. "I am very happy to see such a change."

James! Remain strong!

I remained calm and paced my breathing. She moved the conversation to the Nurse's reports. I guessed she had to try another route.

"Even the Nurse's reports remain positive and promising." She informed. "I am pleased James, very pleased."

James, center your energy...feel my strength...feel the water...

It seemed obvious that Doctor O'Shea was going to spend the remaining minutes of our session testing and denigrating me, but that didn't happen. She picked up the phone and called the nurse's station.

"Can you please ask Frank to come to my office?" She spoke quickly the place the phone down.

Doctor O'Shea looked at her watch. "James, Frank is going to take you down to the Imaging Center. Doctor Swartz has ordered an MRI and EEG..."

I cut in. "Is it necessary?" She knew I hated that machine.

"I don't want you to worry about a thing. Everything will be fine." Doctor O'Shea nonchalantly replied. "The center in Arizona needs to have the latest test results."

I had absolutely no choice but to go through with the tests, yet again. I knew she wanted me to protest and cause a scene, but I maintained my composure and sat calmly in the chair. Doctor O'Shea gave me the option to take a sedative, but I declined. I didn't want any additional poisons within my body.

Frank knocked on the door and then entered the room. She asked me to go with Frank.

"I will see you soon." Doctor O'Shea said goodbye.

I walked with Frank and neither one of us said a word. The silence was so incredibly uncomfortable. I wanted so badly to thank him, and to tell him everything. I wanted him to know that I appreciated him. I wanted to embrace him just so he would know that I would miss him.

I felt it coming—the final, wondrous white *flash*, and nothing or no one could stop it.

The Morning

There's nothing like the early smells of morning. There's nothing, nothing like it at all.
The dew gently places a hand upon its children in such a cleansing ritual of preservation.
"Wake to the early morning sun." Her voice sets the transformation, and it begins again.
Boasting fog crawls rearward and submits its hold to the powerful ascent of the sun.
Calling birds—they wish one another an early morning passage…they open their wings.
Silence slowly recedes as the arms of trees stretch and wave in the meadows.
The Honeysuckle fills the morning air—an element of the grand orchestra of nature.The morning, with Mother Earth's generosity—breathing—Everything is alive.
The morning is Her morning. It is Her copious gift.

June 21, 2009
Sunday 12:39 AM

My dearest Ian,

I hope you find this. I hope you read this letter, and everything within this notebook. I am looking at you as you lay here. You are so precious. You are so much more than I was ever able to express to you. You are an award I never deserved, but one I am happy to have won. This is how I want to remember you. I want you to know that my life has been wonderful. You have been my foundation, and the place I always felt safe. You have completed me.

I wish you could have seen it for yourself. It was so stunning, and my words cannot attempt to describe its magnitude, but for you, I will try. You had closed your eyes tonight as I watched you drift into your own dreams. Ian, the room began to hum and vibrate. It wasn't violent. They were standing at my bed again, and this time I saw their faces. They were smiling at me and I knew who they were. Then there were ones I had not seen before, who entered from different sides of the room. They were gentle and very careful with your body. A thin transparent membrane appeared above you, and then they brought it down upon you. It swathed you completely. It protected you. Then I heard her voice. It was Jade.

I will show you the way, if you wish to come.

The face came down from the ceiling. It was my seal. Jade was my seal. They were one in the same. I felt the connection instantly, and told her that I wanted to go.

Then it shall be.

The five of them dissolved into a silver mist, then the walls transformed into vertical lines of seawater. The other beings—the tall ones, dissolved into one of the walls. The liquid columns continued to grow and build inward, toward me. I kneeled on the center of the bed and waited. I looked down at you Ian, and you were safe. You were fast asleep and remained untouched, unmoved, unaffected.

FLASH

My eyes were blinded for a split second, and then I became consumed by the glass ball. It sucked me inward. The sphere quickly gained momentum and we began a rapid plunge. It was so crystal clear. They were waiting for me. The orb moved me alongside the reefs. Corals of every color opened and waved as I passed by. Fish swam the length of the expanse until the terrain opened below. I saw him. My seal. His breathtaking water dance was spectacular. He came to the glass ball and rested his head on the top. He looked down at me and then closed his eyes. He held the orb...my orb. He was beautiful.

Look and see. You are not alone.

The transparent, spherical vehicle dropped over the seawall, and forced its way downward. It was very dark as it took me further beneath the depths of the ocean. We sped faster and faster...down...down...down.

Look. Look at the place it all began. You have been here before.

At first, it looked like fireflies in an open country field. The blackness was thick, and tiny lights began to rain downward toward me, around me, above me. The depths slowly became full of light...slowly...so slowly. The amount of lights across the space was incalculable.

Do you see? Look again.

I did not know what they were until they began to settle closer. My heart began to beat faster, and a memorable emotion entered my soul. I was not alone. I had never been alone. The miniature lights were other orbs, and within the glass spheres, were people! I never felt such oneness as I did at that very moment.

Now I will show you.

We began to ascend together. The mass of illuminated globes dove deeper with incredulous speed. I continued downward with the enormous group, and without pause, that is when it came into view. Huge whales hovered on either side of it. We were welcomed by their deep bellows and high-pitched cries. The structure resembled an old church, with elegant and octagonal spires. The towers reached endlessly toward the surface like outstretched arms awaiting us.

Almost like a beautiful Queen Palm, James.

Within the center of the formation was an immense and brilliantly lit cavity. Colored lights rapidly soared around the huge gap, almost like a beacon. Each of the orbs began to make their way toward the structure. Those colors, I saw them before Ian! They were not balloons after all!

RED—WHITE—YELLOW—BLUE

We will be waiting for you, James…

FLASH

I reentered my body with such force. I was back here in the bedroom with you Ian. I was kneeling in the center of the bed, just as I was when I was taken. You remained asleep. It is time for me to leave. I can no longer live in this body. I have to go. Please let everyone know that I will always love them, and I will be waiting to see them again. This world is no longer the place for me. You know me better than anyone else does. You know that I am not giving up or giving in. I am just moving on. I am happy, but most of all, I am ready.

I will be there anytime you need me. When you need to feel me, just open your arms. From the shore, you will feel my presence. From the shore, I will always be there to hold you. I will love you forever, because a love like ours goes on and on.

James

…Letting go

It was just after 5AM, and I stood in the CNS lobby. The police were interviewing Doctor O'Shea, while several Staff members waited for their turn. James was gone. He left me, while I slept two feet away from him. I was broken and lost. I walked hopelessly toward the elevator. I looked down at my feet and noticed my tennis shoes. As I walked, they squeaked. They were almost completely soaked. As I continued to the elevator, I was surprised that I hadn't notice my wet shoes earlier. The elevator door closed, and up I went. James took my keys and nothing else. He had left everything behind and vanished from the facility with only the clothes he was wearing. Seconds later, the elevator opened onto the second floor, and I exited. I began down the hallway toward his room. Then I heard it. It was low, but I definitely heard it. It was there. James had the song playing low on the stereo. He looped the song so I would know…so I would never be able to forget. I ran. I ran so fast. I entered his room and turned up the volume. The sound of Celine Dion's, *My Heart Will Go On*, blared loudly, and filled the room. I stood there listening to the song as I scanned the room. It then unexpectedly filled my nostrils. It was the distinct smell of ocean water, and I looked down to see the floor covered in at least an inch of it. I looked over at the stereo again, and resting beside it was this journal. It was opened to the last page. I brought it closer, and read his letter in its entirety. Soon after, I did not realize that I was running again, but I was. Out into the hallway, saltwater began to stream beneath my feet, and toward the nurses' station. With his journal in hand, I bypassed the elevator and jetted down two flights of stairs, and out into the lobby. Doctor O'Shea caught my eyes as I flung through the door. I went over to her, and thankfully, the police were done interviewing her. I quietly asked her to follow me. She had her handbag with her and I made sure she had her car keys. We casually left the main entrance and made our way through the disarray of police officers and camera crews out front. I told her that we needed to go. We made it to her car and she pleaded with me to tell her where we were going. I told her to give me her keys and get in! I pulled out of the parking space before either one of us had our seatbelts fastened. Doctor O'Shea incessantly asked me where we were going, but I did not answer her. I continued to hear the song play inside my head. I knew James was gone, and through this song, his message rang through. It was time for me to let go.

He wanted me to go there. He wanted me to see the sunrise and witness the dawn of a new day—his new day. The day he was set free. I found my vehicle. James was definitely here. I parked her car and I asked Doctor O'Shea to remain behind. She stood outside the car and watched me walk away. She was crying. It was the first time I witnessed a human emotion from her. I continued to walk. The sun was just rising and in the distance I heard them crying. I followed the seagulls along the boardwalk and down the path toward the beach. I did not want to go. I didn't want to face it. I was not ready to say goodbye. What future would there be without him? I knew I had to keep walking. I knew this was his wish and now he needed me to say goodbye.

The Florida foliage began to clear, and just after a patch of Palmettos, the path brought me to the entrance of the beach. I hoped to see him one last time however, that wish faded instantly. I saw his sneakers, his socks, his pants, his underwear, and then his orange

Reese's T-shirt. I walked alongside his footprints in the sand until they touched the surge of incoming water. I was there and James was with me in spirit. I felt the emotions build within my chest. I looked out into the distance and saw the gulls flying high above the water. They were crying so intensely, almost in song. The waves crashed and expanded, and a wash of water encroached upon his footprints—our footprints. Within seconds, the proof of our final walk together was erased. My emotions raged and I couldn't do a thing to salvage that last vision of ours. It hit me like a ton of bricks. I stood there and screamed his name. From within the depths of my soul, I bellowed out into the sea. There was no response. I wanted to hear his laugh…his voice. However, the only sound was the voice of the ocean. I fell to my knees and opened my arms. A warm breeze entered my chest, and I let the incoming tide embrace me. I felt his arms around me, and I cried within his hold. My best friend, my life partner, and my love, was gone. James went home.

James is now one with the blue.

Afterward

Frank soon found employment at a different medical facility in southern Florida. He continues to care for individuals suffering from Huntington's disease, and other brain diseases. Frank became a close friend of the family and remains in contact regularly. The entire family has grown to love Frank as one of our own, and we often celebrate holidays together.

I called CNS and tried to contact Tonya, however I was told that she no longer worked for the hospital. To this day, I have not been able to locate her.

Three months after the investigation, Doctor O'Shea left CNS and set up a private practice in Chicago. She called me from Orlando International Airport the day she left Florida. She and I shared small talk, but her voice said it all. Doctor O'Shea will never be the same. The last thing I asked the doctor was if James ever mentioned Jade. Doctor O'Shea said no, and quickly wrapped up the call. Doctor O'Shea and I have not spoken since, but I remain wary of her silence. I have many questions for her, and the day for her to provide me with answers, will come.

Everyone at CNS eventually found out about the *others*—Liz, Cathy, Mickey, Walter, and Kitty. Liz and Cathy were James' Aunts.

Mickey and Walter were James' Uncles, and Kitty was James' Grandmother. These family members had passed away a long time ago, however James spoke of them as if they were alive. On the other hand, I never mentioned Jade to anyone, until that last phone call with Doctor O'Shea. I never spoke of his journal, or of his dreams, to any of the Staff except for Frank. Who was Jade? What was she? Was she real? The hospital got back with me regarding the 'water' in James' room. They said the water came from a broken pipe in James' bathroom, but I know the smell of saltwater. Sometimes I wonder if I was hallucinating. I often wonder if James dreamt about the sea, or did he truly experience it? Was it the disease? What do we really know about the brain? Did the disease allow James to tap into something most of us only wish we could? Is there something or someone below the surface of the water? If so, who and what are they? His stories and encounters were so descript, moving, and so believable. Personally, I am glad that she was real to James. She was there for him when no one else was. She was there for him when I could not be. For that, I will continue to visit the shore whenever I need to feel his presence…his embrace.

For that, I will always remain thankful to the one he called Jade.

Notes

A few weeks after James left CNS, I received the following four documents via priority mail from Frank. Certain fields were redacted. What were they trying to hide? Frank found a way to copy these documents before the entire file was sealed and archived. Soon after, Frank called and requested that we meet. He drove up from southern Florida and we met in Orlando, at a busy café in Downtown Disney. Frank mentioned that there had been many additional documents. However, he was unable to obtain them securely. Just before he left CNS, Frank said that he and another nurse witnessed the abrupt arrival of four individuals from The Department of Defense. Accompanying them were two doctors and six, fully decorated and armed military soldiers. They held a closed-door meeting there, and for almost five hours, CNS was locked down. All Staff, and every patient from Unit A, were moved to various units within CNS. No one was able to enter or leave the building. When they left, a moderately sized military truck was packed with brown boxes and other items. Frank said these items appeared to be large, but concealed by dark brown canvases. However, before the military crew secured the vehicle hatch, and left CNS property, Frank recalled seeing a silver rim of a bathtub protruding from under an unsecured canvas. I asked him to be completely open with me, and he knew I was gathering information for a reason. Frank shared additional information with me; however, I have decided to keep it to myself for now. I had to admit to Frank that I was not surprised at all. He knew I served in the United States military as a British Citizen and nothing had ever, or would ever shock me. Frank asked me of my future intentions. I told him that this was far from over, and I was biding time. I would wait. I would simply wait.

I returned home later that day from my visit with Frank. I had several errands to run, and then I visited with James' parents for an early dinner. On my doorstep was a small, unmarked brown box. I opened it and inside was a DVD with a short handwritten letter. It was from Frank.

I didn't give this to you earlier today, but you have to see it. Call me when you are done questioning everything you ever believed in!
Frank

Facsimile

Matthew Swartz, M.D.
Chief Neurologist
Head of Neurological Studies
CNS—Center for Neurological Studies

Date: July 06, 2009

Re: James ▮▮▮▮▮
MRI & EEG Test Results

Doctor ▮▮▮▮▮

    This is my second attempt to contact you. I called your office and now I urge you to meet with me and discuss ▮▮▮▮▮ MRI ▮▮▮▮▮ and EEG results. I understand your position; however, after reviewing the results ▮▮▮▮▮ of three independent labs, they have come to the same conclusion. Their assessment ▮▮▮▮▮ ▮▮▮▮▮ verify an unexplainable reversal of reduced volume of the caudate nuclei and ▮▮▮▮▮ Huntington's ▮▮▮▮▮ We must not allow the ████████████ due to James ██████ unfortunate ████████ These finding must be shared with the medical community. This is nothing short of a miracle. We simply have no answer for the reversal of ████████████ A full investigation regarding the ████████████████████ of that night must be completed. It is imperative that we speak soon. I have received notice that ████████████████████████████████ ██████████████████████████ are coming to CNS to remove ████████████████████████ from patient's hospital room, and ████████████. If you wish to observe or sample any of these items, please contact me directly at the Center. It is urgent that we speak. I cannot delay them!

Sincerely,

████████████

Matthew Swartz, M.D.

Center for Neurological Studies
███████████████ Orlando, Florida 32803
Phone: (407) ████████ Fax: (407) ████████

Confidential Report

Date: July 02, 2009
Date of incident: June 21, 2009
Patient: James ████████ Age: 37 DOB: ████████ Diagnosis:
Huntington's disease
Sources: CNS video recordings, and facility Staff statements
Dear Officer ████████████████

Below is a timeline of events as per your request. You will also find the video footage enclosed. Several cameras are placed within the facility; unfortunately, we cannot explain the interference during the captured footage. Our technicians have worked diligently to find the root cause for these anomalies; however, we are unable to provide an explanation at this time.

12:39:55AM—Security Guard, Mr. ████████ is seen on video sleeping while on duty.

12:41:33AM—The patient is fully dressed and stands outside his second floor bedroom. Hall lights begin to flicker. Before complete video outage, it appears that the cameras are sprayed with ██ water.
**Video footage from all floors captures "white-noise."

1:32:57AM—Anomaly clears, and the first floor (side hall) camera shows the bottom portion of the courtyard glass door smashed.
Video footage clear of water (unknown liquid)

1:32:59AM—CNS alarm fails to sound. No clear explanation found by technicians. Alarm found to be working without any technical issues.

1:36:44AM—Outside video footage fails to capture any additional video of patient—James ████████
Video of courtyard shows blurry (faded images)

2:24:34AM—Video footage remains clear—No further anomalies recorded.

2:25:11AM—Footage shows Nurse ████████ waking security guard—

Mr. ███████
2:26:29AM—Nurse ██████ calls Doctor O'Shea from security station (desk phone) in facility lobby.
2:49:53AM—Doctor O'Shea returned to CNS.
* Night Nurse: Mrs. ████████ specifies that she was administering medication to three patients and did not hear the break-in of the office of Doctor O'Shea.*

In her report, Doctor O'Shea indicated that several video recordings and three audio tapes were accessed by the patient prior to his escape from CNS. She is also concerned that her written notes and files were accesses. Please see attached report from Doctor O'Shea for additional information.

Please contact me directly if you have any additional questions. This places CNS in a very difficult position with the patient's family and the State. Please expedite all necessary procedures as quickly as possible.

Sincerely,

Theresa O'Shea, M.D.
Center for Neurological Studies

████████████████████████████████

Date: July 01, 2009

Re: Incident on June 21, 2009
Patient: James ████████
CNS and ████████████████ Police Department

████████████████████

Leading up to the incident on June 21, 2009, James ████████ behaviors of irritability, suspiciousness, lack of self-control, sleep disturbances, and hallucinations, increased. On June 21, 2009, the patient forced his way into my office. Upon examination, the patient scanned through several video and audio recordings of previous sessions. In addition, he forcibly gained access to notes and files, which were locked inside my filing cabinet. According to what I examined early that morning, the patient was exposed to materials with the following information:

(Below are excerpts from prior notes. Complete documentation attached.)

—The patient often experienced delusions.
—After waking from the coma, the patient definitively believed his head injury resulted from a car accident.
████████████████████████████████
████████████████████████
—He also believed the facility was located in Boston, and not in Florida.
—On several occasions, he mentioned seeing snow outside. ████████
delusions continued ████████

—The patient's mental faculties rapidly degraded, and he began to speak of, (and to) the following individuals: "Sarah, Liz, Cathy, Kitty, Mickey, and Walter." Ian ███████ (patient's Domestic Partner), confirmed that Liz, Cathy, Kitty, Mickey, and Walter were names of his deceased Aunts and Uncles.

██

Although abnormal, and blatant signs of ███████████████ these hallucinations never materialized into physical aggressions toward himself or to Staff.

—The hallucination (alternate personality)—"Sarah" was, however, an abnormal and physically aggressive manifestation.

██

personality disorder to deflect his ████████████████████

██

I was unsuccessful with ███████████████████████, and due to current circumstances, I urge for his file to be closed. It is in my professional opinion that CNS handles this matter carefully, however it is the final decision of ████████████ the State, and Dr. Swartz. As per the MRI, we are waiting for the review from ████████ independent lab. I am unable to comment at this time on ████████

██

I am sure you understand that this letter contains private information, and must be handled with appropriate consideration.

Sincerely,

████████████████████████

Theresa O'Shea, M.D.
CNS Psychiatrist
Cc. Doctor Matthew Swartz

Matthew Swartz, M.D.
Chief Neurologist
Head of Neurological Studies
CNS—Center for Neurological Studies

Date: January 10, 2008

Subject: Intake / Critical
Patient: James █████████
Status: Comatose / Head injury
Diagnosis: Huntington's disease

   James Valvano was admitted today to CNS. James was transferred via ambulance from Orlando █████████ James was diagnosed with Huntington's disease on █████████ He had been seen by his Psychiatrist █████████ for nine months and was assisted (at home) by his Domestic Partner, Ian █████ with medication administration. Due to manifestations of advanced behavioral, emotional, and psychiatric disturbances, James attempted to attack his DP in their Saint Cloud home. According to the attached report, James slipped and hit the left hemisphere of his head on a coffee table in their home.

His DP called for an ambulance. Once at ███████████ Hospital in Orlando, Florida, the patient slipped into a coma.

██

Four additional police reports had been filed in the past two years due to patient's outbursts and physical aggression toward DP and other family members. The family understands that CNS will monitor James, however due to the nature of the head trauma, chances of recovery is improbable. As per agreement between family and CNS, CNS agrees to maintain the life of patient until natural death occurs, or until termination of life support is requested by Ian ███████ All medical treatments and costs will be incurred by, and the responsibility of CNS for the remainder of patient's stay.

*Attached documents (medical releases) completed by DP.
*Full medical reports from PCP, and Psychiatrist.
*Intake to be filed at CNS.

LaVergne, TN USA
21 February 2011
217286LV00004B/72/P